Praise for Fal

A Rainbow
Murder Mystery

"Call me a stickle I am and I liked the fact that Sandra Robson's *False Impression* starts off with a body in a dinghy. Can't ask for more of a mystery than that.

"Well, maybe you can. It appears throughout that the murder has to do with Nazi activity off the coast of Florida during WWII and how it affected residents in one small seaside village. But the victim is too young to have been involved. Throw into the stew a wealthy man running for statewide office, brief glimpses of a diary that appear to document locals' entanglement with the Nazis, blackmail, and Robson's book interlocks a lot more than the opening chapter's murder.

"Robson's clean, sharp prose keeps the story moving and by the end of the third chapter, I cared about her character, Keegan Shaw. Robson made Shaw smart enough to get involved with solving the murder when she's thrown violently in the middle of its cause, but kept Shaw from appearing as a super hero.

"Shaw's array of quirky roommates all come off as authentic. And that also includes the bad guys, the cops and those you have to wonder about as the story unfolds. To Robson's credit, she handles the mix of oddball roomies in Shaw's life without cluttering up the story. Quite the opposite, the roommates move Shaw's investigation along.

"*False Impression* is better than a good read, it's a story that the reader gets involved in. Trying to solve the crime before final pages is a tempting challenge. I hope you have better luck than I did.

"Keegan Shaw is a character I hope to see more of."

—Michael Haskins, author of the
A Mick Murphy Key West Mystery series

"*False Impression* made a great impression! Fun in the Florida sun, and a mystery with a little history. Keegan Shaw is one heroine I hope to see more of!"

—Miriam Auerbach, award-winning author
of the Dirty Harriet Mysteries

"Juxtaposing the U-boats and intrigue of the Florida coastline during World War II with today's arts scene, Sandra Robson has crafted a mystery for both ages."

—Sandra Balzo, award-winning author
of the Maggy Thorsen Mysteries

False Impression

A Keegan Shaw Mystery

SANDRA J. ROBSON

Rainbow Books, Inc.
FLORIDA

False Impression: A Keegan Shaw Mystery
Copyright © 2016 Sandra J. Robson

Author's Website: SandraRobson.com
Softcover ISBN 978-1-56825-187-5
ePub ISBN 978-1-56825-188-2

Published by
Rainbow Books, Inc.
P. O. Box 430
Highland City, FL 33846-0430
Telephone (863) 648-4420
Facsimile (863) 647-5951
RBIbooks@aol.com • RainbowBooksInc.com

Individuals' Orders
Toll-free (800) 431-1579
BookCH.com • Amazon.com • AllBookStores.com

This is a work of fiction. While most of the locations in the book actually exist, some are the product of the author's imagination. Any resemblance of characters to individuals living or dead is coincidental.

Front cover image by iStockPhoto
Interior images courtesy of the author
Author photo on the back cover by Cynthia A. Smith
Previous edition © 2010

All rights reserved. No part of this book may be reproduced or transmitted in any form or by any means, electronic or mechanical (except as follows for photocopying for review purposes). Permission for photocopying can be obtained for internal or personal use, the internal or personal use of specific clients, and for educational use, by paying the appropriate fee to:

Copyright Clearance Center
222 Rosewood Dr.
Danvers, MA 01923 U.S.A.

Produced and printed in the United States of America.

For my dad, Donald Thompson, who trained on Miami Beach and served on sub-chaser USS 1022 from 1942–44. And for my mother, Wanda, who spent the early years of her marriage following him to Newport, Rhode Island, Cambridge, Massachusetts, Brooklyn, New York, Norfolk, Virginia and points south.

Other Books by Sandra J. Robson

Mystery Fiction
False as the Day Is Long: A Keegan Shaw Mystery

Self-Help
*Girls' Night Out: Changing Your Life
One Week at a Time*

False
Impression

Prologue

A lady's writing desk sat in front of the sitting room windows. It was a delicate walnut affair with an impressive view of the wide river, but it was only for bills or thank you notes. For writing in the journals, she always chose the table in front of the large gilt mirror.

The mirror was magic. In just a few carefully crafted sentences it not only reflected the past, it transformed it. Wrinkles smoothed away. Hair became darker and shinier. Faded eyes brightened to youthful impudence. Even old-lady slacks and shirts blurred to the slim skirts and padded shoulders of the Forties.

She sat down and opened the journal.

No lights were allowed within ten miles of the shore now, not even in the small towns . . .

False Impression

As the words flowed from her pen, Florida present-day vanished. Gone were the condo-lined beaches, pervasive snowbirds and never-ending boredom.

Instead, it was Florida, 1943: German U-boats skulked the ocean depths, torpedoed sailors swam through burning water to shore, miles of barbed wire lined the coast, and Miami was as cosmopolitan and hedonistic as Casablanca. And the love, oh God, the love . . .

She began to write faster, hurrying to become part of it all before memory failed or, as sometimes happened, she got confused. There was death in the past, but she pushed that thought away along with any other unpleasant truths. Other people's ethics were useless. The truth was, you had to believe in yourself.

And so, in age, as in youth, she remained unaware that her actions might provoke tragedy. Or that recording her personal memories could ever provide a motive for murder.

Chapter 1

Some people never learn, but the Irish are the worst. I mean, if you choke on a powdered donut and have to be rushed to the hospital for a tracheotomy, you probably stay away from powdered donuts after that. Not the Celts. Our genetics are skewed, warped somehow to draw us to the very thing we dread. As my ex husband used to say, as solemnly as if he'd thought it up himself, "Dread and dream are only one letter apart."

Which explains why, on an August morning hot enough to discourage mouth breathing, I was headed for the Riverwalk, a place that held no good memories for me, unless you call being dumped by your boyfriend cause for celebration. The thing is, if you're going to wallow in misery, you should do it staring at a river. It's a lot classier than curling into a ball on the bathroom floor.

False Impression

I rounded the corner of Main Street, walked to the top of the Riverwalk stairs and stared into a solid wall of heat haze. Both river and sky were so shrouded that the houses on the far bank were invisible. All I could see was the plank walkway below, part of city pier and the vague outline of a Trimaran ninety yards offshore.

The Tri had been anchored out there a long time, probably two years, and only a ripple of water off the bow made it look like a boat instead of a fixture. A portion of mast lay lengthwise across its hull.

Off to my left there was a rustling sound and a flutter of something white. I turned my head away and hurried down the Riverwalk steps. Someone was actually here before me, sitting at the picnic table in the park. I walked faster. Talking to people at seven on Sunday morning never makes my to-do list.

At the far side of the band platform I dropped to the weathered planks and dangled my legs over the side. The tide was out, and the river lay like a clear, undulating blanket over green mossy rocks and striated sand. It breathed ancient, placid disinterest in anything besides itself—a perfect place to wallow in wretchedness. I sucked in a chunk of sultry air and wallowed.

The problem wasn't just being dumped by Alex, It was my failure to deal with nine years of marriage to a practicing asshole—oops, alcoholic. After the fatal car wreck—his—I didn't take up skydiving, head for the Galapagos to study birds, write a soul cleansing book or even resurrect my career as a photojournalist. Instead, I hid out at a friend's beach cottage for two years.

I'd like to say I walked a lot, breathed in salty, healing air and developed a backbone, but the truth is I never walked the beach. Mostly I sprawled on it, sometimes in the rain and twice during storms. I was perfectly aware that if the cottage had a name, it would be Womb with a View, but I didn't care. I slept on a fold-out sofa, inhaled junk food, watched *Law and Order* reruns and read boxes of paperbacks. If a pipe hadn't burst in the bathroom and flooded me out, I'd still be there.

Instead, I was sitting here, a 42-year-old widow with no clearly defined destination and no estimated time of arrival. No, not *widow*, I couldn't even get that straight. Jack and I had been divorced six hours when he smashed himself to pieces driving drunk. I was merely an ex. I got up, brushed the crud off my shorts and walked down the pier that extended out to the floating dock.

There was no breeze off the water at all, and sweaty hair stuck to the back of my neck. A rowboat, loosely tied at the far end of the pier, lay perfectly still in the hazy water. Its owner was obviously, cleverly, somewhere cooler. I stared at the boat as I trudged along, and something began to rise up like an anemic moon. It hovered for three long seconds before sliding, bit by bit, out of sight.

I ceased walking. The round white thing looked like a head.

As I hesitated, it raised again—a man's head, with a face the color of school paste. His mouth opened, fish-like, but no sound came out. I glanced back down the pier, but I was the only one around. *Damn, if somebody had fallen, was hurt, I should do something.*

"Help mmm . . ." The whisper barely reached me as the head sank out of sight.

Where the hell was my pepper spray? On the other hand, did I really believe somebody was lying around in suffocating heat just for the privilege of mugging me?

Still, this was south Florida. Well, nearly. I sucked in a breath, walked to the edge of the pier and looked down.

He was lying flat in the bottom of the rowboat, bearded face looking up to the sun. His faded green T-shirt was soaked brownish red around an oozing wound, and Christmas cookies were scattered all over him.

Christmas cookies? Surely not. I squeezed my eyes shut and re-opened them, positive the picture would shift if I could get the focus right. And then I heard my own voice, too loud in the heat-enclosed silence.

"Hold on, I'll get help."

He tried to raise his head, but this time only his chin moved.

"Wah . . . duh . . ." A thinner whisper. He was scrawny and not very clean, and despite the matted blonde hair that touched his shoulders, he looked young.

I reached out to him, stopping short of the ragged wound in his chest. "I'll call the police."

"Wait. Wahd—uh—wahd—uh . . ."

I nodded frantically as blood dripped onto the wood planks. "I'll get water. Hold on." I shot back along the pier, feet thudding on the rough boards. There was a woman in a white shirt sitting up in the park at one of the picnic tables, and I shouted at her.

"Call the police! Call the police! Somebody's hurt!"

She threw down the newspaper she was reading and got to her feet—a girl, not a woman. Then she moved down the grass to the edge of the terrace and shouted back, "What's the matter?"

"Somebody's hurt! Call the police!" I skidded around the corner onto the Riverwalk and crashed into a man carrying a fishing pole and a bait bucket .

"Sorry," I gasped in a ragged breath of humid air. "Didn't see you."

"Hold on, hold on! What's the matter?"

"A guy's hurt out there," I pointed a shaky hand at the dock, "Blood all over him."

The fisherman, who looked at least seventy, eyed me for a couple of seconds before deciding to believe it. Then he dropped the pole and trotted down the pier, still carrying the bucket. I turned to ask the girl if she had any water, but she was at the picnic table, punching something in her left hand.

"Battery's dead!" she shouted down to me. "Have to find a phone!" She ran out of the park.

I realized I was shaking and tried to think. Spike O's coffee shop would have water, but it was two long blocks away.

"Hey!" The fisherman was coming back along the pier faster than he had gone out. "I thought you said somebody was hurt out there."

"He is," I was frowning as he reached me, "in the bottom of the boat. Isn't he there?"

"Oh, he's there all right, but he's a little more than hurt. The guy's dead."

Chapter 2

I had a philosophy professor once who gave a trick question on every final. It read: Life is . . . A. an accident, B. an opportunity, C. a big shit sandwich, and every day you take a little bigger bite. The answer was C. Eventually, he was edged out of the department and forced to teach sociology, which only proved his point.

I'd always considered the sandwich thing unduly negative, but as I stood guard at the mouth of the pier with the fisherman, whose name was Louie Janclowski, I decided maybe the professor had been onto something.

"You come here a lot?" said Louie.

The question, a singles bar staple, nearly sent me into hysterics. *No,* I thought wildly, *only when Alec dumps me for his ex-wife. The wife who gave him the boot, cleaned out his* *bank account and moved a series of tryout guys in and out of the $400,000 house he built for her. Only when he thinks rescuing her is more important with being with me. Only when there's no money coming in, my savings is nearly gone, and the air conditioner is on its last legs. Only . . .*

"Not really," I got a grip along with a normal voice, "just getting a little exercise before it turns really hot."

He nodded. "That's why I fish first thing."

"What's goin' on down there?"

The voice, loud and insistent, came from a kid up in the park. He leaned across the handlebars of a bicycle, one foot on the ground, and looked down at us.

I checked my watch, but it was only a couple of minutes since the girl had gone to find a phone.

Louie Janclowski eyed the bicyclist and growled. "No income, baggy pants, chains in the pockets, loser."

I blinked at him. "Excuse me?"

"Only one goal—guys like him. Hang out and try to make your parents as miserable as possible."

"Is something wrong?" The kid propped the bike against a park bench, walked a few feet down the terrace and raised a hand to shade his eyes. Even from that distance you could see the tattoo on the skin between his thumb and forefinger. It looked like a thick spider web.

When neither of us answered immediately, he said, "There was this girl running down the street. She said somebody was hurt."

Louie frowned up at him. "You see the police coming this way?"

"Police! Hey, no way, man. I don't hang with cops." He hustled back to his bike, mounted it and wheeled away.

An "I told you so" smile flickered around the corners of Louie's mouth.

"Maybe one of us should go call," I said. "Seems like a long time."

He grinned at me and patted his shirt pocket. "I punched 911 soon as I seen the guy. Wife makes me take the cell phone when I fish alone. I'll wait here, you see if anybody's coming."

I started back the way I'd come, down the Riverwalk to the stairs leading to the street, but Louie yelled at me.

"Don't go that way! Too hot. Sidewalk's shadier."

He was right. I took the only other access to the street, a sidewalk that curved up to the left in front of City hall and followed a tree-lined path to the park. There was no sign of the girl, but her newspaper was spread out on the picnic table with a to-go cup sitting in the middle of it. She came running up just as a patrol car, lights flashing, pulled onto the brick pavement behind her.

"I couldn't find a phone," she said, her breath coming in ragged gasps.

"It's okay." I waved a hand at the police car. "Somebody else called them."

"Oh, good." She patted her pockets frantically. "I musta left my cell here."

From the pier, she had looked normal enough. Up close she looked like a responsibility searching for a place to take root. She was thin, too thin, with a face like an angelic boy and silky brown hair cut close to her head. Low-slung, dangerously tight shorts topped her long legs, and a man's white shirt was tied over a midriff-exposing tank top. Three gold rings pierced her belly button, which was probably why her face seesawed between pouty and pained.

The officer was out of the car, walking toward us.

"Somebody call about a body?"

"Down there." I pointed at Louie. "At the end of the pier. In the boat."

He turned and headed for the steps. "You ladies just stick around for a while, okay? Try not to talk about it until my supervisor gets here."

The girl jerked around to face me. "You never said anything about a body, you said somebody was hurt!" She put both hands over her eyes. "He's gonna kill me! Omigod, he's gonna kill me!"

I sat down on top of the picnic table. "Who's going to kill you?"

"My . . . my dad. He hates publicity."

She dropped her hands and watched the policeman who had stopped to speak to Louie. After a minute, the cop continued down the pier, and Louie came up the hill, following the same path I had taken.

"Your dad'll understand you don't go out Sunday mornings looking for bodies. How old are you, anyway?"

Her eyes shifted to me and then back to the policeman. "Twenty-four, but it's not that easy. I'm Jerricha Roddler. My dad's Tom Roddler."

I'm Keegan Shaw . . ." I paused. There was a Roddler involved in state politics. "Not Roddler running for state senator? That Roddler?"

Her mouth twisted a little. "That's me. He warned me to 'walk the straight and narrow' when I moved up here."

I shrugged. "Just tell him you were sitting here reading the paper, minding your own business, when somebody discovered . . . an accident."

"You don't just tell him anything, but thanks. I saw you before, when I was reading the newspaper, but you didn't notice me."

I nodded, watching the policeman who was now kneeling at the edge of the boat dock. "Anything worth reading in the paper today?"

I didn't really care, but she seemed a lot closer to sixteen than twenty-four, and she was probably better off thinking about something besides her publicity-hating father. And I was definitely better off not seeing that awful white face rising up over the end of the pier.

"Huh-uh, not really. Just that." She pointed to a full-color picture of a Mediterranean style house with big SOLD letters across its left corner. The caption read: "After 47 years DeLong house goes to Michigan couple. Editor of 'Sunshine Quarterly' closes shop."

"Really. That is news." I shook my head. "Florence DeLong and that house are Seminole Beach institutions. Most people thought she'd die there."

"No." The girl started folding the paper. "She's going into a condo and putting the money in my dad's campaign."

"Whose money and whose campaign?" Louie Janclowski asked as he arrived at the top of the bank, breathing hard. He set the bucket and fishing rod under a nearby tree and wiped his neck with a grubby-looking handkerchief. Jerricha stared at her platform shoes and didn't answer.

"Florence DeLong," I said finally, in the awkward silence. "She's selling her house out on the point and," I glanced at the girl, "apparently backing Tom Roddler for state senator."

"God, Florence DeLong." Louie sat down on the picnic bench and pulled off one of his waders. "Must be at least a hundred by now. Spent her whole life arguing over things nobody gave a damn about. Big stories about World War II and the exciting things that happened here back then. Hell, nothing happened here. Place was a backwater." He tossed one slimy-looking boot into his bucket. "What's she giving money to Tom Roddler for anyway? He oughta just stay a lawyer and be happy he's got a job. Damned Democrat."

Jerricha's eyes brightened, and she looked directly at him. "She's his mother."

He frowned. "What?"

"She's his mother. Florence DeLong is my grandmother."

"You're kidding." I must have sounded more surprised than the information merited, because both of them turned to look at me.

"It's just funny," I said. "She was on the interview list for a film I'm editing."

I didn't say that I'd called twice for an interview and she'd refused both times. I also didn't say that the film was about World War II in Seminole Beach, since Louie thought that was a non-event.

"You make movies?" Jerricha looked at me with interest.

"No, it's just a college project. Local history, nothing artsy at all."

"Oh." She turned away.

Louie leaned down and pulled off his other boot. "Well, all that money won't hurt your dad any, maybe even buy him a better campaign issue. Haven't heard one word about unemployment or food prices or global warming. All I heard him say so far is how Schwarzenegger should never have been governor of California. That ain't much to run on."

Jerricha grinned at him. "He says nobody should be elected to anything if their father was a Nazi. He says it's a slap in the face to every World War II veteran who gave his life for this country."

Louie gave her a look. "I know what he says. Way he talks you'd think he was there himself. Good publicity I guess."

The girl's smile slid into a frown. "It won't be good if I get mixed up in a mess."

"Nothin' to do with you." Louis shrugged. "You didn't do

anything to the guy, right?" He tossed the second wader in the bucket.

Jerricha looked horrified. "Of course not, but the reporters make stuff out of nothing. Even if they're wrong, and they have to say later that you weren't involved, people go on believing all that shit anyway. Look. The cop's coming back. "Omigod, omigod! What's he going to do?"

All the drama was beginning to wear me down. "Here." I picked up her Styrofoam cup. "Drink your coffee and quit worrying. Just tell them what you saw."

"But I didn't see anything!" She made a face. "This is cold."

"Drink it anyway. It'll calm you down."

The officer came up the stairs to the street, looking hot in his navy-blue uniform. He crossed the grass to where the three of us stood, took out a notebook and looked at me. "I'll need your names and addresses."

"Keegan Shaw. Thirty-two East River Road."

He wrote it down and looked at the girl.

"Jerricha," she mumbled. "Jerricha Roddler. I'm staying with Cindy Meir. On Osceola Street. I don't know the number."

He wrote it down and shifted his attention to Louie. By the time Louie spelled his last name twice and gave his address, another officer and two detectives had arrived. Ten minutes later, the three of us—Jerricha still clutching her cold coffee—were on our way to the police station to give statements, and there were squad cars, supervisors and crime-scene people everywhere.

Chapter 3

I was driven to the station by a detective whose name I forgot as soon as he told it to me, Jerricha rode off in a patrol car muttering "Nothing to do with me," and Louie apparently drove himself. I heard the detective tell him to just follow Officer Smith.

I had to wait forty minutes before being interviewed by Detective De Cicero. He checked my name, address, date of birth, then got down to the serious stuff.

"Sure you don't want a cup of coffee or anything?"

I shook my head. Anybody with a TV knows police coffee stinks.

"Okay, let's go back to around, say, seven last night?" He settled back in his chair. "It's easier to remember if you work up slowly. For instance, what'd you have for dinner?"

24   *False Impression*

Time lines don't take long when you haven't been out of your room for a week. I gave him the short version, but I lied about dinner. Only losers make three courses out of a bag of chocolate chips on a Saturday night.

DeCicero made a couple of notes and looked up at me.

"You usually walking around downtown on Sunday mornings, Mrs. Shaw?"

"No, not usually."

"Any special reason for choosing the Riverwalk today?"

Yes, officer. My boyfriend dumped me, and I have no life. Nobody to read the comics with Sunday mornings, nobody to lie on top of me and finish drying off after his shower, nobody . . .

"I wanted some exercise," I said aloud.

"Okay. So, you didn't see anybody at all until you got to the river and then just this girl, Jerricha Roddler, in the park. You say anything to her? Hello, whatever?"

I shook my head. "I saw her sitting there, but my mind was on other things."

The pace of his questions slowed the closer we got to me finding the kid on the dock. I told him how the head raised up and how he asked for water and about the blood dripping and the cookies spilled around. I felt like I was making it up.

"You didn't see a weapon of any kind in the boat? And there was nobody else around at all?"

"No, well, a guy on a bike. But that was later, in the park after Louie called the police."

"Can you describe the guy? Age, weight, height?"

"Dark hair, not tall, not heavy. Twenties probably. He was wearing surfer pants, you know, the ones that hang off your backside. No shirt. And he had a tattoo." I pinched the skin between my thumb and first finger. "On his right hand. A spider web."

DeCicero made more notes.

"What happened to him?" I said. "The dead kid? What made that kind of wound?"

He spoke without looking up. "We're still investigating. We'll know more after the medical examiner has a look. Ever meet Jerricha Roddler before this morning?"

"No."

"You still teaching communications at the college?"

I blinked at him, wondering how on earth he knew that. *My new friend, Jerricha? Or did he have a file on me? And if so, why?*

"Part time," I said. "A class here and there. A little editing, a video project for a colleague."

He looked interested. "You doing any projects right now?"

"Not really. Well, one, if I can find enough information to make it work."

"What's the subject?"

"World War II in Florida." I cocked my head at him. *Why does he care?*

He made a note. "Ever have Ms. Roddler work on one of your projects or take one of your classes? Ever see her around the campus?"

I shook my head. "Not that I remember. Why? Does she know me?"

"She says no." DeCicero put down the pen and folded his arms.

"Then?"

"It's just that you were very lucky this morning, Mrs. Shaw. You find a man who's been fatally wounded, probably seconds before you arrive, yet all the time you're down there, you don't see anybody at all. You're lucky Ms. Roddler was around that time of the morning and actually saw you find the body. Very lucky she says you didn't do anything but run for help. Because of her, you get cleared as a possible suspect."

"Suspect?"

He grinned at me and leaned back in his chair. "I'm a cop. I have to suspect everybody. Except my wife, because I know where she is. And maybe the Red Chinese. Travel time alone rules them out."

Any other time I'd probably have thought he was funny. There aren't that many cops doing stand up.

"I guess she's lucky I saw her too," My voice sounded childish, even to me.

"True." He eyed me. "There wouldn't have been time for her to get back up to the picnic table if she'd been stabbing somebody down on the dock."

"So what did happen?"

"We'll know more in a couple of days. I don't suppose you'd mind if we looked to see what you've got in your pockets," he said, very offhandedly.

"You want to search me?"

"No, ma'am, just a precaution. Another way of clearing you of any suspicion at all. If you don't mind."

I stood up, pulled out my key ring and tossed it on the desk. Then I turned out the front pockets of my khaki shorts.

"Got a ten dollar bill in my shoe." I yanked off my running shoes, pushed them in his direction, and I'll be damned if he didn't look them over. Then he handed me his card, requested a call if I thought of anything else and offered me a ride home.

I accepted the ride, but the short, silent trip to the house gave me too much time to think. About disembodied heads and blood dripping on sun-bleached boards. As I got out of the unmarked car, I decided I wasn't up for alone time. Everybody in the house was probably still asleep, and I wanted people and conversation and noise.

The sun had finally eaten its way through the haze as I walked the four blocks to Spike O's and the strong cup of coffee I should have had the second I climbed out of bed.

Chapter 4

When I got to the coffee shop, Jerricha Roddler was sitting at one of the outside patio tables with a bottle of yuppie water. She was still wearing the white shirt, but she'd rolled up the sleeves and managed to look cool in spite of the heat. She was also noticeably calmer than she'd been in the park.

I didn't actually see her until I'd waded through the line straggling out the front door, splurged on a large latte and carried it back outside. At that point she called my name.

"Mob scene, huh?" She grinned at me. "Is that why they call it Psycho's sometimes, instead of Spike O's?"

"No," I paused by her table and drank an inch off my coffee, "it's only Psycho's on Friday nights. A local psychologist sits inside for a couple of hours encouraging people to talk about their problems. If you don't have anything better to do, you can hang around and watch them drift in and pretend they're not here for the free therapy."

She sighed. "I love this town. It's so cute."

Cute. I took another healthy slug of coffee.

"You can sit down if you want," she said in a hopeful voice.

I hesitated, torn between wanting to forget the entire morning and owing her something for being my eyewitness. I no longer felt the need for people and noise; the long wait in line had taken care of that.

"I should probably get home. I need a shower and a comb."

She seemed to deflate a little. "You look okay. People with blonde hair and blue eyes never really look messed up, just interesting."

I voted for gratitude, and dropped into the chair across from her. "Where'd you get an idea like that?"

"My dad."

"Who just happens to be blonde and blue eyed himself?"

"Yeah. So, how'd your cop talk go?"

"Not too bad." I leaned forward to get into the little patch of shade the umbrella made. "Thanks for speaking up for me."

"I just told the detective guy what I saw. He was pretty nice." She giggled and propped a platform sandal on top of the table. "He looked in my shoes, can you believe it? But he only kept me half an hour."

I glanced at my watch. "And you've been sitting here ever since?"

She lifted a shoulder and let it fall. "I, well, I don't want to go where I'm staying yet. Cindy has—boyfriends—and they're kind of creepy sometimes. And there's no locks on the doors or anything."

"Is that why you were in the park at dark o'clock this morning? Isn't there anybody else you can stay with?"

"Not really. My dad's in Palm Beach. There's my grand-mother, but that's out."

"Don't you have a job?"

She shook her head. "I used to work at a vet's. You know, washing the dogs and helping the doctor do examinations and stuff, but I hated it. The animals were always sick."

Well, duh. I didn't say it out loud, but I don't exactly have a poker face.

She didn't seem to notice. "You think our names'll be in the paper? 'Cause we were there where he was?"

"I don't know. We were out of there before any reporters arrived, and the police don't release information until they officially close a case. Why?"

"I don't want anybody coming after me. That cop kept saying I must have seen somebody." Her hand squeezed the water bottle, and her eyes shifted away. "But I didn't see anybody. I didn't even know he was down there."

"You didn't see Louie, the fisherman, go by?"

"The old guy? Sure, but that was before. And he came from the parking lot behind me. He didn't go out on the pier, just down the Riverwalk 'til he disappeared around the corner."

"When was that?"

She shrugged. "Ten minutes before you showed up? I get mixed up on time."

"And nobody else? Maybe you were reading the paper and didn't notice."

"No, I'm not a real good reader, and I was looking around a lot. Nobody was down there."

"Okay, then it's easy. If nobody did anything to the guy on the dock, he must have done it himself."

"Himself?" You could see the idea whipping around in her

head, seeking meaning. "But how did he get there? The dead guy I mean."

"Maybe he came earlier; maybe the rowboat was his."

"You mean he hid down there? Just waiting for . . . for somebody to come along? That's so creepy."

"I know." I pushed away the vision of blood soaking through a green T-shirt. I stood up. "Better get going."

"Okay." She had the no-hope eyes of those Feed the Children ads, and I could feel guilt settling into my bones. Even if she was twenty-four, she looked and acted ten years younger.

"Where does your roommate live?" I said, ignoring the voice that warned me to mind my own business. "If it's not too far, I'll walk with you on my way home. You can't sit here all day."

She shook her head. "I'm not going back there."

"Look, there's an empty bedroom at the house." I spoke louder than the voice in my head that warned me to butt out. "If you need a place to stay for the night you can camp out there. It has a lock; nobody will bother you."

She looked up and frowned. "What kind of house?"

"What kind? A big house. The rooms are rented out to artists, and I live in the mezzanine."

"What's a mezzanine?"

"An apartment between the first and second floor. The artists usually have dinner around seven thirty, but it might be smarter to eat out. Our real cook is in New York promoting her cookbook. Jesse, the temporary cook, is on strike."

"How come?"

I sighed; Jerricha was worse than a two year old. "He's a vegetarian, and his favorite dish is summer squash. One of the guys threatened to do something unpleasant and explicit with the next large yellow thing he found on his plate, and Jesse took offense."

"He's the only one in the whole house that can cook?"

False Impression

"I think they all can . . ." I stopped, sidetracked by a sudden mental picture of the kitchen. Artists create, but they do not clean up. Nor do they recognize the pan they created in when it's full of dirty water in the sink.

"They're all kind of doing their own thing," I said. "When Amy was here we had great food. Homemade cinnamon rolls, New Orleans coffee, fresh seafood, asparagus, pot roasts. It's just better to stay out of there now."

"I can cook."

"Yeah, like what?"

She shrugged. "Anything, steak, chicken, pork chops, gravy."

I studied her for a moment. "Well, you could see what Amy left in the freezer and make dinner in exchange for a room for the night if you want." I checked my watch. "It's only ten thirty. If you needed something from the grocery store, I could go get it." I could hear a faint, hopeful note in my voice.

"Okay, maybe I will, except . . . I should go pick up my stuff. At Cindy's." She tapped the water bottle on the table. "You could stop by with me, if you don't mind."

Cindy's house was six blocks from downtown and two streets off the river, a white stucco-on-termite structure with virulent purple trim and a yard full of weeds and fire ants and raggedy bushes.

The place wasn't technically a hovel, but somebody needed to shovel it out every now and then. There were piles of dirty clothes on the kitchen floor, and a number of drawers had been pulled out, rummaged through and left that way. Empty pizza boxes, smeared plates and open containers of peanut butter, milk, jelly and potato chips littered the counter tops.

"What made you decide on Cindy for a roommate?" I said, watching a fly dive bomb the milk.

"She works for my grandmother, you know, typing and stuff for the magazine. Well, she doesn't now because she's not gonna do the magazine anymore, but she like, pays my rent so she can say where I go."

"Hold on, you're confusing me with pronouns. Your grandmother covers the rent?"

"Yeah, but I'm getting a job, and then I'll get my own place." She darted a glance around. "It wasn't this bad when I went out this morning. "Cindy should get somebody to clean up; she's got a lot of money really."

"Yeah?" Clearly, she wasn't spending it on Pine Sol.

"Well, she owns this place. She got it from grandmother." She turned suddenly and shouted. "Hey, Cindy! You home?"

Nobody answered.

Jerricha edged closer to the stairs. "I have to get my stuff. You want to help?"

"Sure, okay." I shrugged and followed her up the narrow steps.

There were two bedrooms on the second floor. Both were small and dark with tiny windows and slanted ceilings. Jerricha flipped a light switch inside the room on the left and stopped dead.

"What's wrong?" I leaned around her and looked inside.

A small hurricane had apparently ripped through the place. The mattress was sideways on the bed and slashed lengthwise, dresser drawers were upside down on the carpet, and clothes had been flung everywhere. I glanced into the second bedroom. It was a mess too, but the furnishings were intact.

"Who'd do something like this?" I demanded. "Are the people who live here nuts?"

"I don't know." Her voice was a whisper.

"Get your stuff, and let's get out of here. C'mon, show me

what to pack."

It took a good ten minutes to get her organized, but eventually we emerged with a bulging backpack and a hanging bag of clothes.

We went down the stairs and out the front door without encountering anyone, but I was wondering if I'd made a mistake inviting Jerricha to stay in the house.

Still, her father's running for state senator, so how bad can she be?

That thought stopped me cold. "You got a driver's license I can look at?" I said to her.

"Sure." She turned big surprised eyes on me. "I can't drive on it, though. Not since the accident."

"Accident?"

"No big deal; nobody got hurt. The brakes didn't work or something and I hit a window—at a Wendy's." She rummaged through an outside pocket on her backpack and handed me a plastic-covered card.

The picture was definitely her, except she looked even younger than she did at the moment. I handed it back with no explanation, and she spent at least three minutes putting it away.

"What's going on?" I said finally. "What on earth made somebody mad enough to trash your room?"

"It's probably Cindy." Her chin jutted out. "She gets funny if she thinks you're hitting on any of her guys."

"If she did that over some guy, she's a wacko."

Jerricha shrugged and picked up her backpack. "She likes to keep her stuff."

Chapter 5

From the journal, February 5, 1943

The beat of the rumba filled the casino, drowning out the clatter of glassware and chatter of patrons.

"Have one of these," the blonde girl urged. "It's a B-29. You'll love it." She adjusted the diamond V, for victory, pinned to her strapless taffeta dress and tried to look more sophisticated than her nineteen years.

The dark-haired girl, five years older and warier, eyed the cocktail glass.

"What's in it?"

"Two jiggers of gin and one each of passion fruit, pineapple and lime"

"I think I'll just stick to champagne."

"But it's *the* drink darling, the most popular wartime drink. It said so in Life magazine."

"All right," the dark girl capitulated, "anything once." She pointed a red fingernail at the B-29, and the waiter nodded and disappeared.

The blonde girl, whose name was Lucy, looked as pleased as if she'd invented the drink herself. She raised her glass to the third person at the table, a thin man in a tailored suit.

"Here's to Miami, it's got everything: rich government bigwigs, European refugees with titles, men in uniform, fun, liquor and—shoes!" She held up one foot shod in a black-silk sandal. "I nearly died when they threatened to ration shoes."

"To Miami," the man said absently, one eye on the nude dancers. There was a trace of foreign accent in his speech. "We might just as well get to business, Lucy. What is it he wants now?"

She tilted her head, still smiling. "A special favor, Ren. One from you and your beautiful boat."

They continued to watch the stage as the dancers kicked themselves into the wings and a short man in a hairpiece took their place. The orchestra began playing "Yes! We Have No Bananas," and the short man roared out his ode to the wartime housing shortage, "No! We have no apartments, we have no apartments today!"

"Let me guess," Rennie raised an eyebrow, "running a friend across to Cuba? One who has, ahem, misplaced his travel papers, say? Or perhaps just a watercolor sketch of the spy station in Jupiter?"

Lucy smiled at him and shook her head. "I said a *special* favor."

His eyebrow rose a little higher. "The band's going to play again. Perhaps you'd care to dance, Lucy darling."

She got to her feet in an awkward move that belied her sophisticated manner, but her voice stayed low and sexy. "Perhaps I would."

The dark-haired girl lit another cigarette and watched them go. When the waiter returned to the table with her drink, she nodded her thanks and leaned back, tapping her foot to the music.

"You look lonely," an unfamiliar voice said over her shoulder.

She rested the cigarette on the edge of the ashtray and slowly turned her head to look him over, taking in the dark, curly hair and two gold stripes on his sleeve.

He pushed the billed hat back on his head and grinned at the expression on her face. "Okay, not lonely. Like to dance anyway?"

"Dying to." She tried a sip of the drink, made a face and got up. The dance floor was thick with uniforms and winter tourists, but they found a nearly empty spot and squeezed into it.

"Aren't you out kind of late?" She gazed up at him, dark eyes amused.

"Not curfew yet." He swung her out in a modified jitterbug, twirling her around and back again, answering in chopped-off sentences. "Plenty of time to sleep. No rest for the wicked."

The orchestra segued into another rumba, and the stage lights flashed from red to blue.

Three numbers later she left her partner and returned to the table, smiling and out of breath. Rennie was sitting alone, staring into his drink, and the blonde girl was nowhere in sight.

"What happened to Lucy?"

"She had a date." His face had a shuttered look. "Are you free for a couple of weeks?"

"I guess so. Why?"

"I was thinking of taking the boat to Seminole Beach. It's a little place a few hours north. I have a house there."

"Since when?"

His eyes rested on her for a moment. "I have several secrets you know nothing about."

"How little is Seminole Beach?"

"One, two thousand."

"I don't think so, Rennie. Sleepy little towns aren't my thing."

"This one has a USO that gets rave reviews from our boys in blue. Big dances on Saturday night, and they bus in officers from the training station."

"Fascinating. What happens Sunday through Friday?"

"Come now, you'll be bored in Miami if I leave. A respectable married woman like you can't be out on the town alone."

She lifted her chin and shook her head.

"Besides," he took a sip of his drink and held it in both hands. "It'll be like a big house party on the SS Buccaneer—a few friends, another couple I know in Seminole Beach. You can stay on board if you don't like the house. We'll take along somebody to cook. Food, booze, fun, a modest dress allowance if you have nothing suitable." He studied her expression to see how he was doing. "What more could you ask? And then we'll come back to Miami and see if the Navy missed us. What do you say?"

"You're sure there'll be a lot going on? I never learned to knit."

"Positive."

"Maybe." She gave him a thoughtful look. "Where do you come from, Rennie? I mean really."

"My dear girl, I was born in Switzerland and educated in Germany. I make no secret of that. And I've been an

American citizen since I was twenty. A good and grateful American citizen, I might add."

"But what do you do? For a living I mean?"

"Europeans consider it rude to ask. We're usually liked for our connections."

"You know what I mean."

He reached over and picked up her nearly full glass, "I came to Miami twenty years ago when the family money was running dangerously thin, bought the Buccaneer, and ran it as a charter until a relative died and my financial position improved. Then I stopped ferrying people about and invested in a little Florida real estate that will undoubtedly double once the war is over. How's that? Enough of my private business?"

She looked back at the dance floor. "You know what I mean. That drink is disgusting, by the way."

He held the B-29 up in a toast. "That's why I like having you around, darling. You reject bullshit out of hand. That and the fact that you introduce me to so many handsome military men."

"You do all right on your own."

"But carefully. It's illegal in this country, you know."He sighed. "Anyway, I have to make a few phone calls and provision the boat. Meet me at the Roney Plaza day after tomorrow. Around ten."

"You're keeping your room while you're gone?"

"Why not? The cabanas are only sixty-five dollars a week, and you meet so many fascinating people. Though now all they talk about are the U-boats and the blackout."

She studied him for a long moment. "Does this little town have bus service, or do we walk everywhere?"

"Darling, I have a car, of course. Waiting in the garage,

longing to be exercised."

"Nice. But do you have gas coupons?"

"I do. You're looking at a certified X."

"I don't believe it. A B coupon, possibly—if you can prove your travel's essential to the war effort. Maybe even a D—although that's for doctors and mail carriers. But an X is just for police or firemen. Or congressmen, for God's sake."

Rennie shrugged and downed the rest of his drink.

"Does this wonder car have tires, too?"

"Four brand new ones."

"Not true." She frowned at him. "Rubber tires are impossible these days. You only get retreads and—retreads."

"Not when you're as well connected as I am."

"Come on, Rennie, where'd you get them? I won't spill, I promise."

For a second he thought he wouldn't tell her, then he shrugged. "A friend, a close personal friend who's in and out of Brazil every other week."

"But the customs . . .?"

"Just as they're landing, a man throws them out the back of the plane."

The girl closed her eyes, and a slow, unwilling smile spread over her face.

"Rennie, Rennie. You do enjoy the war, don't you?"

Chapter 6

Thirty-two East River Road was quiet when Jerricha and I got there. She took in its three floors, bay windows, river view and looked impressed.

"This is a monster house. And it's all yours? Wow, talk about lucky!"

I didn't answer. The house, an ill-timed investment of my ex's, was part of the divorce settlement, along with enough cash to keep me in food and paperbacks for the two years I was in self-exile. I had never lived there and never intended to—until I got flooded out of the beach house.

I unlocked the back door and took Jerricha in through the kitchen and down the main hallway. Her eyes got wider when she saw the red-and-blue Oriental runners, the antique tallboy and the mahogany staircase that wound up two flights.

"So, how many artists live here, anyway?"

"Well, four at the moment. We have a writer, a potter, a weaver and an ikebana expert. We used to have a fake grad student, a psychic, a dancer and a hairdresser who prowled the third floor naked. They didn't work out."

Her eyes widened. "You're kidding, right?"

"Not even a little."

"But how did you get them all—the artists I mean?"

"Long story. When I moved here last year, I rented one room to a friend who wanted a quiet place to write a book. That was Amy. She knew people who worked for the Arts Council, and they wanted rooms for a bunch of grant recipients. Amy thought it was a good financial move."

"And then she cut out on you and went to New York?"

"Just temporarily. She's coming back. Come upstairs. There are a couple of empty rooms on the next floor."

The second-floor landing was twelve feet by eight and meant to be elegant. It cried out for Victorian chairs and gold-framed oil paintings. What it had was a bare, dusty floor, a mini refrigerator full of sodas and four closed panel doors with big, brass numbers. I paused in front of #4.

"Nita lives in number one, and number three is really tiny, but this should be okay." I opened the door and stood back so she could see inside.

Jerricha's eyes went around the room, paused at the black marble fireplace and bay window, and settled on the lone twin bed and beat-up chest of drawers. "Where's all the furniture?"

"Another long story. The whole house was filled with antiques originally, but they got sold off bit by bit." I pointed to the closet. "Sheets and towels in there, along with hangars. There's only one bathroom on this floor; you'll have to share it with

Nita. Sorry about the dust. Amy was the only one who actually cleaned around here."

I handed over the backpack. "If you want, you can check out her kitchen."

She nodded and followed me downstairs.

Jerricha was clearly hooked on cooking. She nearly drooled over the blue-and-yellow tiled worktable, the china cabinet full of Limoges and Amy's fancy machines. I left her fiddling with a cappuccino maker and went back upstairs to knock on doors.

All four of the people currently living in the house were art grant recipients, which provided room and board and made outside jobs less critical. That meant they created—and slept— when they felt like it. I started with our resident writer on third floor, room #9.

Bear, who is one of the best-looking men I've ever seen, answered the door sporting a deep tan and wearing a pair of dark-blue jockey shorts that matched his eyes. Between yawns he said he'd been up all night working on his children's book, an opus called *One Bunny Short*.

I kept my eyes fixed on his face, instead of significantly lower, and managed not to smirk. Writing bunny stories may not be inherently funny, but for Bear—a would-be Hemingway who makes yearly pilgrimages to Key West for inspiration and whose current unpublished works are angst novels based on his two divorces—it's the next closest thing.

His interest in kiddie lit developed when he fell for a 17-year-old, single mom, but even after she moved on to greener and younger pastures, he stuck with the bunnies. I told him about dinner, and he grunted, stumbled back to the tent he'd pitched in the middle of his room and collapsed on a sleeping bag.

As I pulled his door closed, he raised his head up and muttered, "That guy called again, Ben somebody. You didn't call him back."

"Yeah, right. I'll take care of it. Thanks."

Kenji's room was across from Bear's, and he was standing in its open doorway when I turned around.

"Good morning, Keegan. Nobody is dead?"

That was probably just Kenji being funny, but it's hard to tell because he arrived in the U.S. speaking no English. (Bear claims he learned American from old episodes of *Walker, Texas Ranger*.) He also arrived with razor-cut hair, pressed khakis and polished loafers, but within six months his wiry hair was shoulder length and his wardrobe consisted of baggy shorts, black T-shirts and sandals. "American girls do not like neat men," he had informed me seriously.

Anyway, I told him about dinner, and he motioned me into his room. "Come and see new visuals."

Kenji is an expert in ikebana, which most people think means arranging flowers. In his case, it means arranging underwater digital photographs of corals, sea fans, jellyfish and miscellaneous fish. He got successful enough in Kyoto to be offered several arts grants in the U.S., but he chose Florida simply for the weather. "Quiet town, warm," he told me, "quiet and warm better for work."

I stepped through his doorway into a giant computer-simulated aquarium that filled all four white-painted walls. A school of fish circled 'round and 'round the room, swirling in so close you could almost feel the spray from their fins.

"Watch!" Kenji clicked the remote in his hand and pulled open his closet door. Half a dozen smooth white sharks shot up out of his hanging clothes and swept the length of the aquarium, scattering the other fish in their wake.

I jerked back instinctively as they flew by in a swirl of bubbling water, executed a series of acrobatic maneuvers and chased each other back into the closet.

Kenji shut the door behind them.

"That's amazing. How'd you do it?"

"Secret." He grinned at me, pleased, clicked the remote again, and the overhead light came on, dissolving the virtual aquarium. He pulled his shoulder-length hair into a pony tail and held it in one hand. "About this dinner she cooks. I have four pounds macaroni, top shelf of pantry but not—"

"I'll tell her not to touch it."

Nita's door, #1, was still closed, so I went down to the sun porch apartment to find Jesse.

His French doors were open and he was seated at a pottery wheel with a pile of slimy, gray clay and a scowl on his face. He looked hot, but that happens when you tape all the air conditioner vents shut and install your own canvas "air pullers" in the windows.

After a second I changed my mind and slipped quietly back upstairs. Better to explain about dinner fifteen minutes before it happened than invite a lengthy discussion about large yellow vegetables.

Back in the mezzanine, I climbed in bed with my Sunday paper. It wasn't quite noon, and already I'd discovered a body, been questioned by the police and rescued a well-connected waif. Maybe I should go across the street and discuss it with Alec . . .

Reality hit me like a smack in the forehead. For the last hour I'd actually forgotten my ex-boyfriend and his screwed-up ex-wife and whether or not they were in the process of re-tying their mostly convoluted knots.

I went out to the landing that doubled as a sitting room, descended three steps to the glassed-in porch and stared across the street. Alec's second-floor patio looked the same as usual: tile-topped tables, outdoor fireplace, bedraggled potted plants. Except the double doors to his bedroom were closed, and he wasn't sitting outside, feet propped up, motioning me to come join him for martinis.

He's gone, a cynical voice said in my head, *and he won't be coming back.*

A second voice chimed in, sounding pleased. *Better get used to being alone.*

I shut my eyes and turned away before I was forced to gulp down a fistful of antidepressants.

Lots of people have a little voice in their head, a kind, protective voice that alerts them to danger or attacks of just plain stupidity. Not me; I have two, and neither is kind or helpful.

The first sounds like my Aunt Bridget McAlister, a dedicated old maid and never-ending source of negative inspiration who came to live with mom and me the year my parents divorced. "I'll give you something to cry about," or "Just get glad in the same pants you got mad in, missy," was about where she peaked in a crisis.

The other is colder, meaner and more humiliating, the voice of Jack Shaw, my ex, who never caught me doing anything right. One of the best things about living at the beach after he died was the roar of the ocean—it drowned out his constant haranguing. Aunt Bridgie's too.

The sound of the phone ringing brought me back to the present, but I let the machine take a message. The chance of good news right now was minimal.

"Keegan? Pick up if you're there." It was Ben, and I heard him take an audible breath. "Listen, I'm out of town this week, but I need an update on the video. I know this is Joey's responsibility, but he's already left for Greece, and besides, he's related to somebody at the college. Somebody so important he'll probably get the credit, no matter who finishes the

DVD." Silence. "Come on, Keegan, I need you."

More silence, then, "All right, okay, it must be more of a mess than I figured. Listen, just throw something together. Are you listening? Give me thirty minutes of straight World War II in Florida—doesn't even have to be good—but I need that grant money. Look, I'll up the stipend to fifteen hundred. C'mon Keegan, this is slam-dunk for a former hotshot photojournalist. Call me back at least and let me know what you're thinking." He hung up.

I stared at the telephone, irritated. Ben's project was a turkey, and he knew it, but I'd bailed him out a couple of times before, and he wanted another miracle. Too bad. Not my fault if Joey let him down. Ben's close male friends had a habit of doing that.

I got up and went to the kitchen. The material Ben had given me, newspaper clippings, magazine articles and photographs, were piled on the counter. I'd been through it twice, but Joey had used everything he had for a short, unimpressive video which he burned to DVD. Then he quit cold, leaving no outline, no notes and no clue to what else he had in mind. Still, there was no point in continuing to avoid Ben. I shoveled everything back in its original box. Tomorrow I'd drop it off at his office, and he could figure it out when he returned. I shut off the phone, got back in bed and stayed there until dinner.

Chapter 7

Dinner that night was closer to normal than it had been since Amy left. For the first time in weeks, everybody had a clean plate and ate together sitting down. Every scrap of Jerricha's stuffed pork chops, mashed potatoes, gravy and buttered corn disappeared without a trace, and she couldn't have been more popular if she'd ridden into town sidesaddle on a donkey.

Even finicky Jesse seemed happy, and the conversation, fueled by real food and two bottles of Saint-Émilion from Amy's stash in the pantry, also approached normal. Until we got to the part where Jerricha and I had discovered a dying man on the Riverwalk.

Seminole Beach is still a small town, in spite of the winter migration of snow birds and tourists. We have drunks and fights and an occasional knifing, but if people want to kill each other, they usually do it in Miami or West Palm Beach. That was probably why Nita, Jesse and Kenji responded to the story with one part shock and three parts disbelief.

Bear, on the other hand, was all over it and asked a lot of complicated questions neither Jerricha nor I could answer. He insisted on hearing the dying kid's last words so many times, I finally snapped at him.

"Water, Bear, he wanted water. That's all he said. And then his head seemed to get too heavy, and he stopped talking."

The silence that followed lasted about six seconds, then Kenji cleared his throat and remarked, "Human head very heavy; weighs same as bowling ball."

Bear continued to concentrate on me. "Let me get this straight. The cop says the guy was wounded seconds before you found him because blood was still dripping . . ."

Jerricha made an odd sound in her throat, and I shifted in my chair.

". . . but Jerricha's sitting there for at least ten minutes, and she doesn't see anybody, including the wounded kid." His eyes narrowed. "And when you come walking up, you don't see anybody either."

He shifted his attention to Jerricha. "How about this? Some guy runs barefoot down the dock, knifes the kid and hunkers down in the boat. You're reading the paper and don't hear him, and Keegan can't see him from the top of the Riverwalk stairs. The killer waits 'til she goes down the steps and then swims away. It could happen that way, right?"

Jerricha looked confused. "I didn't see anybody swimming."

"How would the runner know there was a guy was out there if Jerricha didn't?" I said to Bear. "Were both guys lying in the boat together?"

He shrugged and poured himself more wine. "Maybe the

kid just tripped and fell on his own knife. Jerked it out of his chest, and it went in the river."

My stomach registered a couple of sharp pains, possibly due to pork grease, and I pushed my plate away. "Can we talk about something else?"

"Good idea." Nita was sitting next to Jerricha, who looked a little queasy herself. "Don't you know anything pleasant?"

Bear frowned at her. "Amy called."

Heads raised up all around the table.

"And?" Nita said hopefully.

"She's doing some cooking show, won't be back for a month."

That was less than terrific news. That meant more non-existent meals, more accumulation of dust, and Bear without a girlfriend or significant other, or whatever they call it these days. Which wouldn't matter if he wasn't too lazy (he would say too busy) to look outside the house for female companionship.

I'd made it clear long ago that he wasn't my type. I prefer men who support themselves, no matter how hot they look.

Nita, who was older than Bear, had always treated him like a sibling, but lately I'd noticed him eyeing her with more than platonic interest. That was probably because the old Nita, a solid 180 pounds with baggy sweats, graying hair and her full share of wrinkles, had started running mornings and put a face lift on her ex-husband's charge card. She'd also lost forty pounds.

The easygoing Nita, with kind eyes, still looked out at intervals, but the external package—the deep tan, streaked blonde hair and spandex shorts—was unsettling. It would be unfortunate if Bear got seriously unsettled before Amy returned. Amy disliked encroachers almost as much as Jerricha's roommate Cindy did.

Kenji had been unusually silent during dinner. Now he cast a sidelong look at Jesse and leaned close to me. "Maybe Jerricha," he slurred the name a little, "stays and cooks?"

I shrugged. "You want a job 'til Amy comes back, Jerricha? It wouldn't pay much, but you could have a room."

"Say yes," Nita said. "This is the first decent meal we've had in weeks. Where'd you learn to cook like that?"

Jerricha's pout became a tentative smile. "A girlfriend of my dad's. She used to let me help, showed me stuff. I guess I could stick around for a few days if you wanted." She was trying not to look pleased. "I don't have anything else to do."

Bear gave her his trademark smirk of approval, and I felt a tinge of déjà vu. Then I shrugged it away. Surely he'd learned his young-girl lesson by now. Anyway, it wasn't my problem. I wasn't the moral arbitrator of the house. If Amy wanted to keep what was hers, she could get herself home and do it. I went for another bottle of wine. Even if Jerricha cooked for only a week, it was better than the chaos of the past couple months.

When I returned, Nita was telling Jerricha about the six-by-ten-foot screens she was embroidering up in her room. "There are four of them and they barely fit through the door," Nita explained. "Don't expect embroidery like grandma used to do. These were commissioned by a Central Florida bank with a lot of offshore investors and even more blank walls. They want running visuals of the Seminole Wars—and they want blood."

Jerricha looked suitably impressed, and Jesse, not to be outdone, offered to show her how to throw pots on his pottery wheel.

Jesse has thin, sandy hair, a matching moustache, and he loves everything: clay, herbs, the sky, his pots, the sun porch, even his narrow mattress-bed on a box against the wall. I've often wondered if he was released early from a place surrounded by barbed wire.

Bear, who loses interest when the conversation shifts away from him, interrupted with more questions about the dead guy. "Look, the cookie thing," he said, frowning. "Why Christmas cookies in August?"

Kenji turned to look at me. "Keegan, you smelled, uh, cookies?"

I shook my head. "Why would I?"

"I mean, was strong smell—in air around?" He raised a hand, palm out. "Crack cocaine cookies smell very distinct."

"Oh, yeah?" Bear hates it when somebody knows something he doesn't.

"Yes." Kenji nodded. "Make cocaine thick liquid and pour in Tupperware. Gets hard like Christmas cookie before you cut shapes."

Tupperware? I stared at him, thinking he seemed to know a lot about it. *Maybe it isn't just macaroni he has squirreled away in Amy's pantry.*

Nobody seemed in a hurry to leave the table, and in the spirit of détente I went to the kitchen for a fourth bottle of merlot. When I returned, Bear was asking Jerricha about her grandmother.

"I saw Mrs. DeLong was selling her house," he said. "Quite a place, built in the twenties?"

Jerricha wiggled in her chair and looked bored.

"Paper says bad luck house," Kenji remarked. "One owner has heart attack. One dies in jail. Next has cancer in Chicago." He glanced sideways at Jerricha. "Bad luck house so grandmother buys for low price. Not afraid of very big house?"

Jerricha seemed to understand every word. "I guess she wanted a lot of room for the magazine."

Bear kept at it, using open-ended questions and many one-syllable words, but all he got was shrugs and grunts. Jerricha did admit to being Tom Roddler's daughter, to being a soccer star in high school and to finding her grandmother's magazine "like so crashy," which appeared not to be a good thing.

"She's quitting anyway," she said finally. "She's too old."

"What is she, seventy?" said Bear.

"Eighty-something. She thinks vitamins make her look younger, but they don't."

He shrugged. "Just good genetics, huh?"

Jerricha shook her head. "I don't think she takes that; it's the Preparation H. She puts it all over her face before she goes anywhere and—*whap*! The wrinkles all get sucked up, just like that."

It was after ten when I decided I'd had enough to drink and headed up to the mezzanine.

Bear caught me in the hall.

"How well do you know this girl?" he demanded in an undertone.

"Not at all until today. Why?"

"Well," he paused for effect. "I think she's lying."

"Yeah, about what?"

"I think she did see somebody down on the dock."

"Then why not say so?"

Bear raised his head and looked down his nose at me. "Because it was probably somebody she knew. Somebody close to her. Like family."

Chapter 8

At three the following morning, the air conditioner took a dive.

The entire house was jolted awake by a combination of screeching, grinding and banging noises. When those finally gave way to ominous silence, nobody went back to sleep.

I was downstairs in the kitchen at five, all the windows wide open, searching Ben's box of materials for anything that would translate to thirty minutes of videotape and the down payment on a new air conditioner. There was less than a thousand dollars in the household account, the rent check for the artists ($2,400) wasn't due for another three weeks, and the last guy who serviced the cooling system warned that he couldn't fix it anymore.

I hate owing money so much, my one and only credit card

was in the freezer, encased in a plastic water jug. Ben's $1,500 looked like the only solution.

Jerricha, wearing cutoffs and a top so tiny they almost weren't there, was also in the kitchen and as crabby as I was. She had pulled all of Amy's cookbooks off the shelves and piled them on the work table.

When I asked why, she scowled and said she was organizing them by colors. *Colors.* Amy would be thrilled.

Kenji, who preferred working in his room, was downstairs pacing the floor and making growling noises in his throat; Nita sat at the work table waiting for coffee and worrying aloud that her tapestries were getting damp; Bear shouted down from upstairs every couple of minutes—mostly four-letter words in various combinations to protest everything; Jesse did not appear, probably because his "air puller" was keeping him cool on the sun porch.

I don't think well in extreme heat or emotionally charged situations. I grabbed the morning paper, my coffee and Ben's box of materials, and went to the garage. My aging BMW is a little beat up, but the air conditioner is a trouper. I put it on full blast, made myself comfortable in the front seat and sorted through the box again, one item at a time.

There was only one long-shot possibility to get the cash: an interview list I'd rejected earlier because most of the people on it were already featured on Joey's DVD. The three that weren't, I'd ignored, since NO had been doodled over each name in thick black ink. I shoved the list in my pocket to decipher later. Then I picked up two fat, squarish art pens from the bottom of the box that had probably been used to do the doodling. Old Joey had flashy tastes in writing implements. Except one was wider than the other and not a pen after all.

I admit I'm technologically challenged. Blue Tooth, to me, means an alarming need for dental work, but I know a Record button when I see one. I punched Play and let it run while I opened the newspaper to see if the dead kid on the Riverwalk had made the front page.

He had. The police identified the body as 26-year-old Robbie Garcia, a Seminole Beach native. Garcia's half-brother, whose name was not given, hadn't seen Robbie for nearly a year and didn't know where he was living or working. A half-sister, also unnamed, could not be reached for comment. Garcia had a criminal history dating back nine years, including arrests on charges of selling marijuana and prescription drugs, burglary and fleeing a police officer. No weapon had been found, but police were calling the death suspicious and would continue investigating.

I folded up the paper. Marijuana and illegal pharmaceuticals. Kenji was probably right about the cocaine cookies. The good news was there was no mention of Jerricha or Louie or me by name, which meant no curious phone calls from friends, neighbors or assorted weirdos.

Thunk! Thunk! The sound was so loud and so close, I nearly had a stroke.

Kenji's eyes, inches away, stared into mine through the driver's side window. I rolled it down with a shaky hand. "What the . . . ?"

"Bear writes sitting in toilet," he announced in a belligerent voice, his accent thicker in his anger. "No one can go in."

I was tired, irritable, and my eyes were already narrowed to slits. "Use the second-floor bathroom, Kenji."

"Nita is there. All my stuff upstairs. Must go teach class." He continued to stare at me.

I turned off the air and got out of the car, wishing for the twentieth time that Amy was back. She had a knack of calming the inmates, mostly with one-syllable words ending in k.

Infighting wasn't my strong suit.

Kenji followed me up to the third floor as if he were afraid I'd escape, and Jerricha trailed along from the kitchen. Jerricha was tiptoeing, for some reason, but the sound of Bear's old manual typewriter was louder than her bare feet. When I got to the open bathroom door, I called out. "Bear?"

"Yeah? What? I need quiet here, not a damned parade."

No shit. I stepped over the door sill. He was sitting in the bathtub, water up to his waist, leaning toward a Royal typewriter that rested on a plastic stool.

"And don't ask me why I'm working in here," he snapped. "It's too damned hot in my room, and I can't afford to get behind schedule. Let me know when you've got the air back on."

Schedule? There's a schedule for unsold, un-agented bunny books?

"Nobody can use toilet," Kenji protested.

"Go ahead, use it. Won't bother me," Bear began pounding on the Royal.

Kenji's eyebrows shot up nearly to his hair line.

"Yo, Bear!" I raised my voice over the racket and attempted to channel Amy. "Find somewhere else to work on the bunnies."

He stopped typing and glared at me. "I'm writing a mystery. I'm working out how that guy got murdered yesterday. Classic, locked-room stuff, and I need quiet! And cool!"

I stared at him for a second, trying to decide how to get him out of the bathroom. Better yet, out of the house.

"Okay," I said. "Total waste of time, though."

Bear glanced up, blue eyes suspicious. "Yeah? Why's that?"

"Because you haven't profiled the victim. You haven't talked to his relatives or teachers or friends. You haven't even been down to see where it happened. It's all character development these days," I shrugged, "unless you're writing for tabloids. You don't need character for that."

Silence.

A calculating look replaced Bear's doubtful expression.

More silence.

Then, "Well, the Riverwalk would be a hell of a lot cooler than this." He stood up, totally naked, and reached for a towel. Rivulets of water slid down his body onto the typewriter and the floor.

I backed out of the bathroom. "All yours, Kenji,"

On the way downstairs, a lascivious grin slid across my face and refused to go away. Bear might be a flake and a pain in the ass, but in a world where parts are parts, his were exceptionally fine.

Small victories breed self-confidence, and I took it as a sign. I pulled the doodled up interview list out of my back pocket, sat down on a step and studied the three names that had been rendered unreadable. The first looked like Eileen or Ellen Cortes—or maybe Coates—with no phone number and Park Place penciled in beside it. No help there. The second was "L. J-" something, with several letters I couldn't read, and "ski on Drescher Street." I filled in the missing letters mentally and came up with—Janclowski? Janclowski? How weird was that? Could the fisherman I'd met on the dock Sunday be a guy Joey wanted to interview? It was possible, Seminole Beach is small, and Louie looked about World War II age. I glanced down at the third name: "F. DeLeon"—no, "F. DeLong."

Florence DeLong.

Damn. Even though Mrs. DeLong was considered the expert on Forties Florida and good for an hour's worth of video all by herself, she'd already refused to talk to me. Apparently, she refused old Joey too. Maybe she wasn't good at interviews; maybe she was shy.

A brilliant idea slid into my hot, tired mind. Mrs. DeLong might be leery of strangers, but she'd probably be thrilled to chat with someone who'd rescued her granddaughter from a dangerous, fly-infested dump and given her gainful employment. A couple of hours spent picking the brain of a grateful old lady could easily translate to cool air for the rest of the summer.

I stopped in the mezzanine, called Ben's number at the college and lied to his answering machine. I said I was sorry I'd missed his calls, and of course I accepted his offer of a $1,500 stipend. I repeated the $1,500 part twice so there wouldn't be any confusion later. I assured him I was researching and writing, even as I spoke.

Then I went down to the kitchen.

Jerricha had returned all of the cookbooks to Amy's shelves and was slumped in a chair with her bare feet on the worktable. She was holding her silky brown hair up off her neck with both hands as sweat trickled down her neck.

I grinned at her. "You look hot. Want to take a nice air-conditioned ride?"

Chapter 9

From the journal, February 20, 1943

"I want to go too. I love cruising at night."

Rennie shook his head. "I'm taking the airboat, not the Buccaneer, and you won't like it at all. The wind will ruin your hair, and the bumping will make you sick."

"Then take the Buccaneer instead."

"Not tonight," he said in a distracted voice. "I'm keeping a low profile. A lot of people may be donating their pleasure boats to the government, but I don't want mine refitted with machine guns."

"It's dark out. Who'll know?"

"Not tonight, darling."

"But there's nothing to do here . . ."

"Eileen's coming by in a few minutes."

"Oh, right. You and Clyde go out on the town, and we girls just sit at home and play checkers."

He grinned at her. "Not exactly. Clyde and I have an errand, but we'll bring you back a surprise. In the meantime, help Eileen with dinner."

"I didn't come up here to be somebody's maid. Anyway, I don't cook."

"You won't have to. She's making some kind of fish stew. You can go to the basement and pick out the wine. I showed you how to open the door, remember?"

"I didn't go down there. Is it cobwebby and creepy?"

"Not at all, quite habitable . . . nice, actually. There's a full bar and a sofa that makes into a bed."

"But Rennie—"

"My God, can't you entertain yourself for a few hours? I'm serious, no more arguing. Get the wine, help Eileen in the kitchen and put on one of the new dresses we bought. Orders!"

She stood frowning a long time after he'd gone but eventually wandered over to the bookshelves that hid the basement door and fumbled for the catch.

People said there weren't any basements in Florida, but this was definitely below ground. Still, it looked more like a hotel room than a basement. The walls were painted thick cream, and a brown, plush sofa sat against the far wall. There were no windows, but you thought there were, because full-length, brown curtains covered another wall. A third wall was taken up by a long mahogany bar that looked like it belonged in one of Miami's private clubs. The only other furniture was a rattan table and four cushioned basket chairs.

She found the wine rack and chose two bottles at random. Cocktails were the thing these days. Wine was for peasants, but

Rennie always insisted. She took both bottles to the kitchen and went to her room.

In the bathroom she removed her make-up and then, slowly, carefully, put it all back on again. She brushed out her dark hair and pinned it on top of her head with silk flowers, changed her mind, combed it out, and let it fall loosely to her shoulders.

The hair made a perfect frame for her face. She turned from side to side, smiled, frowned, pouted. Each time the mirror flashed back smooth, peach-tinted skin and dark, thick-lashed eyes that melted in the light from the wall sconces. It was a glowing, mesmerizing face, and she never got tired of looking at it. Sometimes it was hard to believe it was hers.

She stared into the mirror for a long time then draped a silk scarf over her hair and pulled on a white-silk shantung dress with short sleeves and an above-the-knee hemline. Once the shoulder pads were adjusted, she stood in front of the wardrobe mirror and studied her body from every side.

What a waste. When you look this good you should have someplace exciting to go, not be stuck in a block-long town with pitiful stores and two decrepit buildings they called hotels. Rennie tricked me into coming here. There is nothing to do in Seminole Beach except eat.

She heard Eileen arrive with the fish and other assorted parcels, but she didn't bother coming out of the bedroom. Her red nail polish wasn't quite dry, and Eileen knew her way around Rennie's house better than anybody. Instead, she stood at the dresser, glanced at herself in the mirror every now and then and flipped the pages of a Collier's magazine. Only when the polish was bone dry did she drift out to the kitchen to check the progress of dinner.

"Oh, good, you found the wine. Is there any coffee? I was

hoping for a cup. Why are we having fish stew? Why not steak or a roast or something?"

Eileen gave her a sideways glance and continued adding wine to a large, white kettle. She turned the gas burner to simmer. "Meat requires stamps and points, and Rennie's fresh out of influence at the moment." She pointed at the shelf over the sink. "The only coffee is that new, instant stuff. You'll have to boil some water."

The girl frowned before she remembered not to. "Maybe I'll just have wine until Rennie gets back and makes cocktails. I suppose you know exactly where they've gone." She didn't bother to keep the displeasure from her voice.

"Not really." Eileen kept her eyes on the stove. "I don't ask questions."

"And what's the surprise Rennie's bringing back from this oh, so secret place they're going?"

"Beats me. He just said have something ready to eat because the cook was taking some time off."

"She doesn't work a hard schedule, does she? We only got here three days ago."

She eyed Eileen's dress. It was obviously new, a flowered two piece, but it didn't do anything for her. It was cut wrong, for one thing. Still, she might appeal to some guys, if they liked big legs, bleached hair and dark roots.

"I think I hear the boat." Eileen continued to stir the stew. "You want to go look?"

"No. If it's them, they'll come where the food is."

Eileen put down the spoon and went out of the kitchen. The girl poured herself more wine.

She was still sitting there when the older woman returned, followed by her husband Clyde and a smiling Rennie.

"There you are, darling. We're back. No more anxious

waiting. You remember Clyde, of course."

"Where's the surprise?" She looked down the hall behind him and saw nothing.

"Having a much needed hot shower." Rennie looked at her appreciatively. "You look lovely, darling."

He went to make cocktails and returned in a few minutes carrying a tray with five glasses. Four were martinis, one a mug of beer. He held the tray out to Clyde, who took the beer, and was handing each woman a stemmed glass when a sound came from the hall.

A tall man with blonde hair and blue eyes stepped through the open doorway. He wore pleated, cuffed slacks and a white shirt, with rolled up sleeves, that looked like one of Rennie's.

"Ah." Rennie handed the man a martini and lifted his in salute. "Our new house guest. Welcome to Seminole Beach." He took a sip of his drink and made introductions.

If Rennie said the man's name, the girl didn't hear it. The cocktail stopped halfway to her mouth as his blue eyes came to her, hesitated, moved on, and came back. Something in the room, the light possibly, shifted, and she was looking at the mirror reflection of herself again—only this time through his eyes. For a long moment his face, like the mirror, held her; she couldn't look away. Then she forced a polite smile and murmured, "Nice to meet you."

The martini seemed heavy in her hand. She put it down and watched the other three, but nothing seemed to have changed for them. Eileen continued to stir the fish stew, Rennie tasted it and made suggestions, and Clyde sat down at the kitchen table, put his head back against the wooden chair and closed his eyes.

The girl nodded and laughed and made an occasional comment, but she didn't need to talk. She was totally in her body, totally in command. She could do nothing, say nothing wrong.

Every time she snapped her fingers, smiled at a joke, tilted her head or sipped her martini, she was aware she did it perfectly.

And every time she did any of those things, the blue eyes of the new guest, whose name was Thomas, stayed with her.

Chapter 10

Coaxing Jerricha out to her grandmother's house was not the brilliant move I envisioned. Mrs. DeLong greeted us, if you could call it that, in a room filled with cardboard packing cases. She was neither shy nor grateful, more like an irate barracuda.

"I expect you back at Ms. Meir's by tonight," she commanded. "I suppose I should be happy you're not lying dead somewhere, since I had no idea where you were and neither did Ms. Meir. She called here several times. Very upset." She stepped sideways as two skinny guys wearing PRIME MOVERS shirts entered the room and toted one of the packing cases away.

"I've got a job," Jerricha kept her eyes on her platform shoes. "Cooking for the artists at Mrs. Shaw's house. I'm not going back to Cindy's."

"Mrs. Shaw's house?" Florence DeLong switched the steely look to her granddaughter. "I'm sorry, Mrs. Shaw, but I've heard of you, and cooking for a gang of artists isn't my idea of career advancement."

Her eyes shifted back to me. "Get us some iced tea from the sun room, please. They haven't packed the glasses yet."

I didn't goggle because I was finally getting used to her communication style; she stared fixedly at one person while she spoke to the other one. It was odd and unsettling, which was probably why she did it. When you're eighty-plus it's harder to control people. I wondered if she'd make eye contact when there were just two of us left in the room, but the answer was no. With two, she talked to the wall.

"You probably think I should thank you for taking my granddaughter in," she remarked as Jerricha stuck out her lip and sulked her way out into the hall, "but you have no idea what you've stirred up. She's a terrific responsibility. Always has been." She didn't seem to mind if the girl heard or not.

I shrugged. "She didn't have any place else to go."

The skin on her forehead moved as if she wanted to frown, but nothing happened. Somewhere in her past there was at least one face lift.

"I pay good money for her to stay with a woman who works—used to work—for me. She belongs there." The corners of her mouth turned down a bit more as the claws inched out. "Ms. Meir doesn't cater to Bohemian or cult types, you see. Some people regard that as a little low class, although it may not mean much to you."

I laughed out loud. I couldn't help it. She wasn't my grandmother, and if she got really nasty I was pretty sure I could outrun her.

"Jerricha didn't just disappear," I said to the side of her head, "she left Ms. Meir a note."

"It didn't say where she'd gone." Her eyes blinked a couple of times. "Jerricha needs structured, clean surroundings, someplace where she isn't lured into any trouble."

"Have you seen Cindy's house lately?" I said, mildly irritated. "Never mind what goes on there. Your granddaughter's a pretty girl, and she spends her time out on the street because your buddy Ms. Meir has boyfriends."

Mrs. DeLong turned and actually looked in my direction. "You mean they bother her? I don't think that's right. I want to sit down." She glanced around as if a chair might gallop up and present itself. When none did, she crossed the room to a black grand piano and leaned on it.

In her slim, white jeans, long-sleeved, black-knit top and gold, hoop earrings, she could have passed for twenty years younger. Her hair was thick, silver and had been cut by somebody who knew how. It was only close up that you realized her shirt had been padded to cover that hollowed-out look old people get, her eyes had faded to a lackluster brown, and every five or six minutes she suddenly ran out of steam.

I glanced around the room she referred to as the atrium. It looked more like a front porch on steroids and felt like a sauna. All of its crank-out windows were open, and it was probably a hundred degrees inside.

Time to sneak away, find Jerricha and give this up as a bad idea.

"I hate moving." Mrs. DeLong said suddenly. "It's worse than dying." She looked down at a large painting propped against the piano leg. In it a dark-haired woman in a red dress leaned on a bar before a wall of bright, busy color. "You're not young at eighty-one, you know." She paused, waiting for me to say she didn't look that old.

I let her wait.

"It's not like the old days." Her eyes moved along the row of photographs on top of the piano, maybe twenty of them, mostly black and whites and mostly of Mrs. DeLong in her heyday. Even in the studio portraits that had blurred to brownish gray, her face glowed smooth and young, her eyes sparkled with life, her hair was thick, shoulder length and luxurious.

In one enlarged snapshot, Mrs. DeLong, in a sailor hat and short skirt, dangled her legs off the hood of a '39 Club Coupe. In another she posed in a two piece bathing suit and smiled over one bare shoulder. In a third, Mrs. DeLong and a young blonde girl, both clad in strapless cocktaili dresses, sat at a nightclub table with an aristocratic-looking man.

There was only one small, colored picture of Jerricha at maybe age ten. It looked out of place in the midst of all that sepia-colored nostalgia.

Mrs. DeLong reached out to a studio portrait of a pale-haired baby boy. "That's Tom." Her finger moved from the baby to one of a good-looking guy with blonde sideburns and the polyester suiting of the seventies. "My son. I knew he'd be something special before he was even born. With the right help, he'd have been governor years ago."

"What kind of help is that?" I said, curious in spite of myself.

"The kind a man gets from a wife who puts him first." She raised her chin. "The woman Tom chose to—marry—was not a great help to him. I've never been a fan of incompetence or lack of initiative."

A sound came from the doorway. Jerricha stood there empty handed. "They already took the glasses," she muttered.

"No." Her grandmother's voice was flat. "They were told specifically how and what to pack. "Go look again." Jerricha melted away, her face mutinous.

Mrs. DeLong drew herself up and looked around the empty

room. "I'm too old for this." She blew out a long, exhausted-sounding breath. "I understand you're trying to help, but she's—Jerricha's different. She's not like my son, who is extremely intelligent. Or even like her mother, who at least went to college. I used to try—when I realized—to help, you know, play games, dominoes or cards, but she always ended up screaming, knocking them off the table. Always difficult. After a while you just give up."

I moved to the jalousie window and looked out, uncomfortable with the sudden shift in tone and what I saw as a poorly disguised bid for sympathy.

"There were always problems." She stared at the picture of her son. "Terrible grades at school . . . and that group of people she got mixed up with. She has to be told what to do. That's why I put her at Ms. Meir's. I thought I was doing a good thing, getting her away from that element, making sure she didn't spend her money on those—"

"Look, Mrs. DeLong," I turned from the window, "I shouldn't be taking up so much of your time. I thought you might be interested in helping with a documentary we're doing about Seminole Beach during World War II, and I brought Jerricha along to say hello. But I can see you have way too much going on right now."

"Don't patronize me, young lady." She snapped it out, but her eyes had returned to the photographs. "What documentary? I thought . . . who exactly is making a documentary about the war?"

"The history department at the college is sponsoring it."

"But—what does that have to do with you?"

"The person they hired didn't finish, and I got the job. I've got his notes and some taped interviews, but . . ."

"Certainly not. I told that young man no the first time he

called with his ridiculous questions." Her head swung back and forth in an agitated manner. "And I know nothing about any interviews. But that's neither here nor there. What we're talking about is Jerricha and this ludicrous cooking idea."

"Hey, I offered Jerricha a job, and if she wants it, she'll get her room and a small salary. It's just doing the shopping and cooking two meals a day. It's up to her."

"It is *not* up to her." Her eyes were furious. "I've gone out of my way to explain it to you. Everybody in the family has tried to help. She's lived with her father and with me, even with a cousin for a time, and God knows where else. She always says she wants to change, and two weeks later she's back out on the street. You couldn't possibly imagine."

"You're probably right, but I gave my word. I'm sorry I interrupted your move." I turned to go and was halted by a sound that would have been a growl in somebody younger.

"I was not finished. If you are so im—"

I waved goodbye without turning around and hustled out of the atrium before she got revved up again.

In the hall I met a furious Jerricha.

"There aren't any glasses out there!"

"Never mind. If you're ready to go, tell your grandmother goodbye."

The car seats were so hot they burned the back of my legs. I backed carefully around the moving van and out into the long, gravel drive, rolling to a stop in front of a separate stucco building a hundred yards away. Like the main house, this structure was a little Mizner masterpiece with cream-colored stucco, red-tiled roof and colonnades. It had a double garage below and what had probably been servants' quarters above. I edged the car under a huge, split banyan tree that shaded one whole end of it and turned off the ignition. The breeze off the river was almost cool.

I sat there and watched my $1,500 drift away. All I had left was Louie Janclowski, if that was actually the name on my paper, and Eileen or Ellen somebody or other. Maybe I should just call up Ben, retract my offer and drive to Walmart for half a dozen window fans.

Jerricha opened the passenger door and jumped into the front seat. "She's really mad at you!" Her eyes glittered. "Only my dad has enough balls to talk back to her, but he never has to, 'cause he's her baby." She muttered something else under her breath.

"What?" I shifted gears and pulled out onto the black-topped lane.

"I said she scares the shit out of me."

"I could see that."

"Well, she seems all fuzzed out and everything, and then she jabs you when you're not sure," she said, suddenly touchy. "You're lucky she's not in your family. Did she ask if you played the piano?"

"No."

"She does that to people all the time. She thinks it's funny." A frown creased her forehead. "She didn't ask you?"

"Nope. What's funny about playing the piano?"

"She glued down the keys."

"You're kidding."

"No, she says she loves the way pianos look but she can't stand the sound."

The word wacko filled my head. I kept it off my tongue.

"Oh, well, one less thing to move. Nobody wants a dud baby grand."

"Oh, she'll take it. She loves that piano." Jerricha made a face. "And anyway, she has to have someplace to keep all those old pictures. She's got boxes and boxes of old stuff. Some are my dad but most are just her. Paintings too. A big, fancy one used to hang over the piano."

"I saw it. She's wearing a red dress?"

"Yeah, the one with all the pirates. I liked it when I was little. She won't let them pack it; she's taking it herself in the car."

"I didn't see any pirates, just somebody leaning on a bar."

"If you look really hard, the wall behind the bar is full of them. You know, eye patches and swords, wooden legs—all that stuff." She glanced over at me. "I'm sorry you talked me into going to see her. I always hate it. Now she knows where I live."

"So what? You think she's going to kidnap you out of the house?"

Jerricha's lip jutted out. "She's mean, that's all. And she'll tell my dad where I am. And he'll show up to have a talk with me. How much could it pay?"

"What?"

"How much could I get for cooking?"

"Oh. Not a lot. How about fifty a week since you're getting a free room, and then we'll see? That sound okay?"

"It'll help." She grinned at me, and her whole face lit up for a second. "She just cut off my allowance."

Chapter 11

From the journal, February 22, 1943

The girl leaned back on her elbows, chin tilted up to the right, and fixed her eyes on the far corner of the ceiling. "Is this right?"

She had practiced the pose in the bathroom mirror, so she knew her jaw line and neck were perfectly smooth. Her skin had been velvety in the light of her vanity mirror; in the basement it would be flawless. She felt the slow smile that spread across the blonde man's face but pretended not to notice.

He put down the brush and walked over to the bar.

"Perhaps a little more . . . like this." His hands closed over her bare shoulders, and he twisted them gently to the left. "And the head." He cupped her chin in the palm of one hand, lifted it slightly, and slowly released it. "There."

"Don't you think I'd look better against the drapes?" She said in a throaty voice. "I promised Rennie I'd sit for you, but this isn't much of a background. Do you really see me posing against a bare wall?"

His blue eyes were amused. "No, I see you posing before a wall of pirates."

She raised an eyebrow but stayed in place. "You're dreaming."

"True. First I will paint you, and then I will add what is needed to make the dream real."

"You're putting pirates in the picture?"

"Of course. There were pirates in Florida, were there not?"

"I don't know, I never heard of any." She pushed shiny, dark hair back from her face. "Florida doesn't have much history. Not like up north."

"But it does," he protested. "Spanish conquistadors came here looking for gold. Florida cow hunters ferried beef to Cuba during the Civil War. In the twenties there was smuggling—rum, I believe—from the Bahamas, and—"

"No kidding." The girl interrupted, pointing across the room "What about that wall? Is that part of Florida history too?"

He returned to the table and began mixing paints. "That wall is my own record, a way to keep track of things of interest." For a second he studied the rough outline of the Florida peninsula and the small clusters of submarines along its shoreline. "But pirates are better. I will put you in the midst of them, and perhaps myself. I will thrust you under one arm and carry you away as plunder."

Warmth spread out of her throat and down through her arms and breasts. She moved her head back to the proper position and made her voice casual. "It'll take a lot of paint to do that—and time too. More time than you probably have."

He stroked the brush through a daub of bright yellow paint, added a touch of black and began mixing it into a larger amount of red. "Rennie is generous with art supplies." He indicated the tubes of paint and the brushes lying on the round table. "He keeps boredom from me, should my business take longer than expected."

"Is it taking longer?" It came out more abruptly than she intended. "I mean, how long before you . . . need to go?"

"A week, at least, possibly two." He moved toward her again, noting the flush on her face and neck. "The color is very good, but you must not move." He reached out to adjust her chin, and a spark crackled between his hand and her throat.

"You shocked me." Her voice was so low it was almost a whisper. "You must have scuffed your shoes on the carpet."

"I don't think so, but there is a way to check." He leaned forward, one hand on her bare shoulder, and brushed her lips with his.

"Definitely a reaction. It must be your shoes. Perhaps we should take them off—to ensure there are no more shocks." He bent down, pulled off her red mules and set them one at a time on top of the bar.

"Now we will see." He held his forearm an inch away from hers. "Oh. Still a great deal of electricity. Perhaps the dress also."

He slid a warm hand down her bare back. "It is a scientific fact that silk is a conductor."

Chapter 12

The two days following our trip to Mrs. DeLong's house were long, unproductive and sweaty. I called the Louie Janclowski in the phone book twice and left messages, but he didn't call back. Eileen/Ellen Cortez/Coates wasn't listed, and there was no street called Park Place on the Seminole Beach map. I went through the box of materials again, with no new results, and wasted a couple of hours trying to find voices on the fountain pen that was really a tape recorder. Eventually, I took the recorder and Joey's abandoned DVD and went up to Kenji's room.

He was sitting in front of a laptop computer, in shorts and no shirt. His frizzy hair was twisted into a knot off his neck.

I held out the DVD. "I've seen this before, but I'd like to look at it again. You mind playing it on one of your computers?"

He eyed the disc. "This helps get cool air?" When I nodded earnestly, he took it out of my hand. "One moment."

It was actually five moments. Kenji's room was painted a dozen shades of white, and its few furnishings were also white: steamer trunks for storage, a state of the art sleeping bag and an old-fashioned dental chair that doubled as an easy chair. I sat cross-legged on the floor while I waited. I refuse to watch movies lying in a dental chair. It's a personal thing.

"How much longer?" Sweat slid down my back in rivulets.

"Okay." He clicked off the lights, and we both leaned forward to stare at the laptop.

At first there was nothing but gray, then huge, slanted letters, like the old-time news reels flashed across the screen in grainy black and white: FLORIDA AT WAR. The letters pulsed, then faded slowly to a guy with a dark ponytail, discontented eyes and a do-rag on his head. He was slumped in a director's chair, elbows resting on the wood arms, chin propped on interlaced fingers.

"That's a guy named Joey," I said to Kenji. "I think he's trying to be Geraldo Rivera."

"No," Kenji shook his head, "your Edward R. Murrow, maybe. But more—more healthful. You know him? World War II? Thick cigarette smoke?"

"No, yeah, well, sort of. He broadcast out of London during the Battle of Britain."

Joey, looking important, began speaking in a husky, authoritative voice:

"In nineteen thirty-nine, the world outlook was bleak. Japan had invaded China, and the Germans had marched into Czechoslovakia and Poland. Europe was in peril. To Americans still dealing with the Great Depression, European happenings seemed too far away and not their concern. At home, money was tight, but there were signs of economic recovery. In Seminole Beach, new local construction provided jobs for dozens of men."

Another black and white banner flashed across the screen: 1940 BEGINS A TUMULTUOUS DECADE.

Joey, looking ominous, let the words of war drop menacingly from his lips: Blitzkrieg, Fall of France, Belgium, Dunkirk, Poland, Hitler, Mussolini, Axis, Italy, Germany, Japan. Without much change of expression, he launched straight into sailfish tournaments in Seminole Beach and the new town theater, which featured *The Thief of Baghdad* on Thursday nights. This was followed by more interviews:

"My dad bought a brand new car for eight hundred and fifty dollars," a man in a billed cap reported. "You got a pound of coffee for thirty-three cents, and a haircut was about a quarter. They started spraying the mosquitoes that year."

A heavyset woman with an overload of blue eye shadow said, "When they opened the new servicemen's club in the Victory Arcade, we were all junior hostesses, and we danced with those cute officers from Camp Murphy down the road. It was a great spot. Right on the river."

The 1941 segment ended dramatically with Pearl Harbor and a local son who had been killed during the Japanese attack, then another black and white banner: 1942, A YEAR OF RECKONING—Florida Fisherman Arm for War. This time the subject was German U-boats.

'They patrolled in packs from Jacksonville to Miami," one man said, "sunk forty-three ships, all told. Down-played it in the papers," he looked disapproving, "didn't want the whole country to panic, but we sure knew about it. You'd see those tankers burning off the coast for days. One night a torpedo hit the reef and knocked some guy right out of his bed."

More stories followed—of merchant seamen swimming through burning oil to get to shore, small planes flying reconnaissance, and sports fisherman fitting out their boats with machine guns.

The film ended without warning, and I glanced at my watch: exactly nineteen minutes.

"So," I said to Kenji, who was still staring at the computer's blank screen, "what's your professional opinion?"

He shook his head. "Too Star Trekky. Needs car chase."

I held out the fat recorder I'd mistaken for a pen. "See this? I pushed play, but nothing happened, and I couldn't find any tape."

He almost rolled his eyes as he took it out of my hand, punched a bunch of buttons and handed it back. "Play again. These kind erase badly."

I thanked him and went back downstairs.

The mezzanine was just as hot as the third floor. I shed my clothes and flopped naked onto the bed to think. I had nineteen minutes of tape from Joey. If I took Ben's thirty minutes of requested programming literally, I was eleven short, which meant five and a half minutes of chatter from the mysterious Eileen/Ellen Cortez/Coates and another five and a half from L. J—wski, who I might have met down on the pier Sunday. If I could find them . . .

At 6:15 I quit thinking about it, put on a sleeveless dress that didn't touch any of my parts anywhere, skipped underwear and went downstairs to eat.

Jerricha produced an impressive baked meatloaf that tasted more like pâté, broccoli with a light cheese sauce and some addictive potato puffs, but tempers were frayed. We ate in a silence relieved only by sounds drifting in the open windows: car doors slamming, babies crying, motorcycles roaring by and glass breaking somewhere close by. I ignored it all, inhaled a second helping I didn't need and was back upstairs on my bed in twelve minutes flat, bloated, hotter than before and wondering if death was actually as bad as most people thought.

When somebody banged on the lower mezzanine door fifteen minutes later, I stayed put and yelled in the direction of the stairs.

"What?"

"Somebody broke in." Jerricha's frantic voice screeched up to me. "They trashed the sun porch and all Jesse's stuff while we were eating."

Well, that explains the sound of breaking glass.

I jumped up and grabbed the sleeveless dress. By the time I got down downstairs, Jerricha was flapping around like she was having a seizure.

"They broke his window out," she wailed. "They could've got in the house. What're we gonna to do? Will the police come again? Omigod, what're we gonna do?"

Chapter 13

Spike O's coffee shop was very cold and quiet the next morning, a marked contrast to 32 East River Road, which featured ninety-two degrees on all three floors, an even higher degree of tenant irritability and a still-frantic Jerricha breathing through her mouth and locking the doors after everybody.

Jesse fed her cups of tea laced with some strange herb he grew himself and assured her the break-in was just kids looking for video games or computers. But I don't think she got the message; she wasn't a good listener.

Jesse's papers and personal effects had been tossed around, but several shelves of pots and sculptures, an expensive kiln and two pottery wheels were untouched. When he opted not to report the break-in, I agreed. It wasn't worth seeing our names on the police blotter over a few bored teenagers and a little broken glass, especially since they hadn't entered the main part of the house.

However, the break-in made me realize that open windows were asking for trouble, even in Seminole Beach. I liberated my credit card from the freezer and called the AC repairman. He promised to show up before noon, but I wasn't waiting around. I was going to find Louis Janclowski whether he liked it or not and then hunt down Park Place and Eileen or Ellen whatever-her-name-was.

Fortunately, Jerricha volunteered to wait for the repairman. All she wanted, she insisted, was to stay inside all day cooking and cleaning, no matter how hot it was. That seemed excessive and possibly compulsive to me, but it wasn't my job to see she had a balanced life.

I grabbed Joey's interview list, a notebook and the fat voice recorder and drove to Spike O's for a small black coffee. Given my current cash-flow levels, it would be years before I tasted another latte.

"Ever hear of Park Place?" I said to the waitress as I ordered

"Monopoly?" She looked at me doubtfully.

"I think it's a street here in town."

"Oh. I don't know. I just moved here from Massachusetts."

Uh-huh. I took the coffee to a table and flipped through the local paper, which looked even smaller than it had the day before. They kept shrinking it a quarter inch every month hoping nobody noticed. One of these days they'd deliver a pamphlet.

I was looking for an update on Robbie Garcia, but there wasn't one. In fact, it was one of those days when they should have just printed NO NEWS in ten-inch letters and saved everybody the effort. Even my horoscope was lackluster. All Aries were advised to think before they spoke. Right. I gave up and pulled out the interview list to re-check Louie

Janclowski's address. Then I turned the page sideways and looked closer.

In the bright lights of the coffee shop, the giant inky designs covering the page didn't look like scribbling, more like ornately printed letters. In fact, it appeared somebody had scrawled "Majorcan dol" the length of the paper, which made no sense at all. I squeezed my eyes almost shut and looked through my lashes. This time the letters spelled MAJOR SCANDAL.

That was interesting, if true. None of Joey's research was even faintly scandalous.

In the meantime, Louie Janclowski lived about six minutes away on Drescher Avenue, and I intended to drop in on him unannounced. It wasn't the polite thing to do, and Aunt Bridgie would have been appalled, but Aunt Bridgie wasn't living in simulated hell with a bunch of irate, possibly unstable artists.

The entire downtown seemed to be sleeping as I went out to my car. Seminole Beach in August: lightning, mosquitoes, a hurricane or two, and everyone with brains as far north as they could afford to get.

I drove slowly in the direction of Drescher Avenue, snapping on the pen-sized recorder and hearing nothing but silence. I left it on anyway. If Joey had written "major scandal" in those fancy letters—and it was his list—had he actually uncovered one or was he just drumming up intrigue for a basically dreary video?

I turned the radio to the oldies station and heard "I can't get no-o satisfaction" come blasting out. For a couple of minutes, Mick and I were in total agreement.

The voice that interrupted my song wasn't loud, but it was very clear. It took a second before I realized it was coming from the mini-recorder. I turned off the radio and listened to an old, thin voice that I was pretty sure I had never heard before.

". . . they will tell you nothing like that happened, but they were children then, and some of them are important people now. You know, the ones that were ten or eleven? They didn't really know anything about it, only what their parents told them. The ones who really remember, like me, are gone."

"You mean dead?" That was Joey's voice.

"No, they went to North Carolina." The woman's voice was flat.

"The people who remember the war moved away?"

"Well, some did. Most of them died, I guess. A lot of my friends died, you know. I just kept on going. My hair was black until I was seventy-nine. I didn't even have as much gray as my daughter. And I never dyed it either."

"Yes, ma'am. I can see that, Now, about . . ." Joey hovered between impatience and affability, "this smuggling during the war?"

"Oh. Well, they did, you know, all kinds of things."

"Like what?" Joey produced a small, fake laugh several decibels higher than his earlier voice. "Somebody told me the only smuggling around here was in the twenties. You know, liquor during Prohibition."

"Well, my daddy did see a whole case of VAT sixty-nine out there in nineteen forty-two, and he said 'I better have that.' "

"You mean scotch? In nineteen forty-two? Not the twenties?"

"No. Yes. And they got canned food and rum and flour. It was all just going to sink anyway. Even the young boys went out there in canoes. Clyde's cousin Louie was smuggling stuff at ten years old. Some of the fisherman would set out their nets and go aboard and throw things over."

"Wait a minute, wait a minute. Are you talking about the merchant ships that were sunk off the coast by German submarines?"

"Oh, yes. Those boats burned for weeks." Her voice trailed

away. "And sometimes they brought in all those poor boys who'd been burned." Silence. Then, "There was plenty around to drink during the war. I was, let's see, I was nineteen in nineteen twenty-eight."

"Okay." He was clearly lost but playing along. "Okay, so you were thirty something in the Forties, right?"

"Yes. Those were wonderful times. All those handsome service men around and the dances at the USO. I was a junior hostess, you know. They all wanted to dance with me. But I liked to dance with Clyde, even if he was 4-F."

"Is that where you heard about the smuggling? At the USO?"

More silence. Then, "No, they all came from Camp Murphy . . . down the road . . . they didn't know anything about it. They had all the upper-crust soldiers down there at the signal school. Well, really it was a radar training center, but that was top secret. A lot of the girls married those boys. Saturday night we'd all go on a bus down there, or they'd come up here. No, they wouldn't have sneaked gasoline or food out to the O-boats."

"You mean U-boats?"

"No, O-boats they called them. They sunk a lot of ships, you know, especially in nineteen forty-two. Once, my friend called, and we took food and men's pants and shirts and went out to the beach, and they were all coming ashore in lifeboats . . . all those men covered in oil and freezing. An O-boat did that. And it sunk a ship a day for weeks. We didn't approve of that, of course."

"No, of course not. Um, you said that somebody here—in Seminole Beach—Americans?—were selling provisions to the German U, um, subs? The subs that were sinking American ships?"

"Well, then they didn't have to go all the way back to Germany. It's a long way underwater to Germany. They never found out who was doing it. They used air boats, so the sonar couldn't pick it up. We had sonar then. But they were no good in rough seas, those air boats, had to be a nice ocean for that. They're all dead now, you know. Clyde died . . . and he went overboard when he was getting away, and Sawgrass just drank himself to death. Rennie went to jail . . ." Pause, then a laugh. "But they got one of them out anyway. Picked him up and got him right out of the country under their noses. Rennie said so. Rennie said he was a good guy, not one of those others. The good Germans always hated the Nazis."

"They got who out? The Nazi, er, German? Was it this Rennie?"

"No. Rennie, he died in jail. It was terrible."

"Okay, who did they get out then?"

"Th—" there was a clicking noise, and the voice was gone.

Chapter 14

I punched several tiny buttons, but nothing happened. In frustration I tossed the gadget in the passenger seat next to my purse. That must be why Joey doodled "scandal." But was it legitimate, or had the woman just enjoyed having a young man ask her questions and made it up as she went along? In the years I'd lived in Seminole Beach, nobody had mentioned smuggling during the war, but World War II wasn't typical cocktail party chatter. Still, if there were any kind of local collaboration with the Germans, people would have known and talked about it. As soon as I spoke to Louie Janclowski, I'd go by the library and see what the newspapers from the early Forties had to say about it.

I turned on Drescher, started checking house numbers and pulled up in front of a white frame cottage with Bermuda shutters angled out over the windows. A hefty woman in red shorts was pointing a hose at some rose bushes, and she told me to follow the path around the house to Louie's shop, which I did.

Louie Janclowski was sanding a piece of light-brown wood, and he peered at me over a pair of battered half-glasses. "I know you."

I nodded. "Sunday, on the dock. I apologize for just turning up, but you didn't call me back. I wanted to ask you a couple of questions."

"I don't call anybody back. What questions?"

"Your name is on a list of people to interview about the Forties. For a video the college is making."

"Yeah? What happened to Fancy Pants?"

"Who?"

"The hot shot movie maker in the muscle shirt. Looked like some damned rapper. Spent a lot of time throwing the word documentary around, like I'd be impressed. I kept him standing out in the sun long enough, he wished he wore a hat instead of a knotted kerchief." He grunted. "I told him, and I'll tell you, it's all a load of crap. I was born right here, and nobody sold the Germans one damned thing or invited them home for dinner either."

"Did he say they did?"

"Oh, he heard rumors. Rumors about everything back then. Bunch of people so far from the real war they just made things up. There wasn't any black market. No spies sneaking ashore to go to movies dressed like nuns. No blue-eyed German soldiers sneaking into family reunions to eat home cooking and not saying a word so they wouldn't get caught. And nobody delivered bottles of milk to the German subs every morning either. All a lot of crap."

"Where did he get those ideas?"

Louie shrugged impatiently. "After he talked to everybody else in town, he started interviewing people so old they couldn't remember what they had for dinner."

"Who?"

"I ain't saying who. I'm just saying leave her alone. Her mind wanders, and that's all I know about it." His lips clamped together, and he glared at a piece of black sandpaper while he folded and refolded it.

"Okay." I shifted feet. "Not much breeze out here. Sure wish I was wearing a hat."

A tiny grin pulled the corner of his mouth, but he didn't look at me.

"So," I shifted my feet again. "What did go on around here during the war? I read somewhere there was a coast guard auxiliary. Did people actually carry machine guns on their boats?"

"Sure, lots of them did." Louie put down the sandpaper impatiently. "Everybody around here did what they could. It was all volunteers. My brother flew for the Civil Air Patrol. He used to land out on the island and listen to the Germans yelling at each other from the U-boats. And my dad was an aircraft spotter for the Homeland Defense. He wore an armband, a blue-and-white armband. I was eleven, and he let me go with him."

"How—you mean people just hung out on the beach and watched for planes?"

"Nah, too many sand flies and mosquitoes. Nobody lived out on the island then. They built a spotter's platform off the causeway bridge that jutted out on pilings into the river. It had a pitched roof in case it rained and a black Bakelite phone. If any plane flew over, you pushed a button, and it connected you straight to Miami. They knew where you were and logged it in."

"Did you watch for planes at night too?"

"Nah, they had two and four hour watches, and my dad used to go out there about three in the afternoon."

"What if no planes went over?"

"Oh, we did a little fishing. And I used to count the cars coming over the bridge. Wasn't much traffic, and the only way to the island was that one wood bridge. Two cars could just about pass on it. You could only go about five miles an hour on it."

"I'm surprised people drove around at all, with rationing and all the restrictions."

"Well, things weren't that bad. You had to paint the top half of your headlights black, and you couldn't drive near the ocean after dark, but you could get around a little. Depended on what kind of sticker you had: A or B or C. C was a good one. My dad had one of those. Sometimes we'd drive out toward Lake Okeechobee. The roads were pretty much empty, and you could get there in about forty minutes."

I nodded. "So, the Homeland Defense watched for aircraft from the river. Who guarded the beaches?"

"Coast Guard. They had mounted patrols—on horseback. And guard dogs."

"And they never caught anybody coming ashore or anything?"

"Nope. They barbed wire, a hundred and some miles of it. Nobody came ashore who wasn't supposed to during the war."

"No German saboteurs around? No spies?"

"Well, now, we had the prisoners, those POW guys in the camps. They were Germans. They worked in the fields, and anybody who had any pull got 'em for nothing. But they came in on a bus, and they never escaped or nothin'," He shook his head. "I'm telling you, none of that stuff ever happened."

"Okay." I grinned at him. "Since, uh, Fancy Pants is no

longer involved, would you be willing to say all that on a video? Kind of set things straight?"

His eyes narrowed. "Put on a damned suit, I suppose, and sit there like a dummy."

"Not unless you insist."

I got the tiny grin again. "Maybe. I'll think about it." The grin turned to a frown. "Americans felt safe back then, you know. Whole ocean between them and Europe. But they woulda been scared to death if they knew what went on in Florida."

I nodded. "You can say that too if you want. Okay if I check back with you in a couple of days?"

"Yeah, I guess." He went back to his sanding, and I watched him for a minute, waiting to see if we were finished. Then he said, "How'd you like that DeCicero down at the police station?"

"He was all right. I don't think I helped much."

"Can't help at all when it's druggies."

"Somebody said all those cookies were really cocaine."

His head snapped up. "That so? They were in the box then, I guess."

"I didn't see any box."

"It was floating under the dock. You were running so fast you probably missed it."

"I guess so. It was pretty awful."

Louie stopped sanding and looked me in the eye. "Not as awful as what those druggies do to innocent people."

I nodded, said I'd give him a call and followed the graveled sidewalk around the house to my car. He was pretty sure the spy stories were bullshit, but it aggravated him all the same, especially the part about the old lady. Five to one she was the one on Joey's recorder. Ten to one she was Ellen/Eileen on Park Place who hadn't appeared on the DVD.

Up to now, my interest in Ben's project had been lukewarm and spurred only by necessity. Now I felt a stir of excitement. There's nothing like a scandal, even a mild one, for turning boring historical footage into must-see footage. If I listened to the tape again, ignored the old lady's confusion over O boats and U boats and people and dates, maybe I could nail down some actual facts. It might be possible to scrap Joey's entire nineteen minutes and replace it with something more exciting than high school football and ten-cent haircuts. I got in the car, turned on the ignition and reached over to the passenger seat.

My purse was right where I'd left it, but the recorder was gone.

By the time I got it through my head that it hadn't fallen out of the car or slipped under the front seat and that someone had actually lifted it, the lifter was long gone. I trotted back up to Louie's back door and pounded on it until his wife appeared, but she hadn't noticed anybody around except a kid on a bicycle. All she remembered about him was "he had those baggy pants that fall off your backside."

I thought of the kid in the park—the one with the tattooed hand—shouting down to Louie and me, but there were lots of kids riding around town with their butts showing. There wasn't one reason to suppose this particular one was following me around trying to steal miniature tape recorders. If I got paranoid enough, I'd be seeing Web Boys behind every bush.

There was no point in calling the police; they'd just ask why I hadn't locked my car. Smarter to swallow my irritation, concentrate on finding Ellen/Eileen and get the story first hand. Since she wasn't in the phone book and Park Place wasn't on the city map, that meant a trip to the courthouse to look through records . . . unless . . . I'd planned to go by the library anyway, maybe I'd just Google her while I was there.

I don't own a computer, but I can surf the Net with the best of them—particularly if there's a librarian close by for back-up. Unfortunately, all the computers were in use, and there was a twenty-minute wait. The historical research corner, on the other hand, was deserted. I settled into a comfortable chair and looked through old copies of Florence DeLong's *Sunshine Quarterly*.

She'd written a number of interesting articles between the years 1941–1945: a story about the POW camps Louie had mentioned, one about the radar training station at Camp Murphy, another describing the secret spy station just twenty miles south. I copied several to read later then moved to the microfilm drawers and scrolled through back copies of the *Seminole Beach Sentinel*.

Nineteen forty was pretty tame stuff, but in 1941 and 1942, the war heated up and the headlines grew blacker and taller: HUNDREDS OF SHIPS SUNK! PROTECT THE COASTLINE! STOP THE SMUGGLING OF FUEL TO SUBS!

Nineteen forty-four was tucked neatly in its little white box, but 1943's container was empty. I went to discuss it with the research lady.

"Somebody deliberately took it," she said, half disgusted, half resigned. "You can't check them out."

"Who'd want it?"

She shook her head. "You never know what people will do. I'm sorry, but we had only the one copy. You might try the Palm Beach or Miami libraries. They probably covered some of our local news then."

"You don't know where Park Place is, by any chance?" I said to the woman, who still looked mad about 1943.

"Yes, of course. I had an aunt there for a while. It's out on the island in the old Shephard mansion. It's an elder care facility."

"Oh, right, thanks." I vaguely remembered the Shephard place changing its name a year or so ago, and Park Place certainly had a classier ring than what most locals called it: the Loony Tunes Inn.

This was not good news. If the old woman on the voice recorder was the one Louie had been talking about, Joey's second unused source was probably senile, or worse.

By the time I got home, the AC repairman was nearly finished, and the house was definitely cooling down. That put a smile on my face, but only until I saw the bill for parts and labor. The repairman told me he'd been able to keep it going this time—emphasis on *this*—but if we so much as sneezed on it, it was a goner. The amount due was staggering. Ben's promised stipend was now nearly gone, and I had yet to earn a penny of it. I signed the charge slip with a sigh, took my copied articles upstairs and dived into the shower.

Dinner that night was ham, navy beans and corn bread slathered in butter. Oh, yeah, and fresh cherry cobbler with vanilla ice cream.

Bear arrived late, but in a good mood, and he and Kenji seemed to have resolved their bathroom issues.

Both of them had seconds of everything, and so did I.

Three nights of heavy food in a row left me feeling so miserable that I asked to run with Bear and Nita the next morning at a quarter of six. Then I went straight upstairs to lie down. The mezzanine was cooling down, and eventually I turned off the TV and flipped through my copied Florence DeLong articles.

They were amazing. Jerricha's grandmother might not be a hotshot communicator in person, but her stories were page turners. One, titled "Hell in Paradise," was about a POW camp located forty miles west of Seminole Beach. At its peak, it housed over 400 German prisoners, most of them U-boat crew captured in the Atlantic. Many were Hitler's finest personnel, and an equal number were hard-core Nazis. The two factions detested each other, according to Jerricha's grandmother.

Mrs. DeLong told the tale as if she'd been there. She explained how the men, many of them technology experts, were forced to cut sugarcane and pick oranges instead of doing the research and scientific experiments they'd trained for. And how they lived with rain, mud and heat and rattlesnakes. And of one eighteen-year-old who was so homesick and depressed that he escaped and committed suicide in the swamp. It was a bit on the bleeding-heart side, and I found it difficult to work up much sympathy for an enemy who torpedoed unarmed merchant ships and, unlike American POWs, ate extremely well in captivity. Still, she did make you see that teenage escapee in stark detail, hanging from a live oak tree, smeared with mud and covered in puss-filled ant bites.

I flipped through a second article, about Miami Beach in 1942, and was immediately sucked into frantic Forties nightlife. Nearly half of Miami's available hotel space had been taken over by the military or military dependents, but even war hysteria failed to put a dent in the city's nonstop partying. Miami was the divorce capitol of the U.S. in those days: 10,000 divorces a year and only ninety days needed to establish residency.

I stopped reading and listened. Somebody was rapping on my downstairs door, and it didn't sound like they were going to give up easily. I dragged myself away from the night clubs, gambling casinos and swaying palms of the Latin Quarter and went down the back stairs to see who it was.

Jerricha stood twisting a kitchen towel into knots. "I told you he'd come here," she hissed at me.

"Who?"

"My dad. He wants to see you."

I started to say no, tell him to call first, and then thought, *What the hell? It isn't like I am doing anything.*

"Yeah, okay, all right. Put him in the great room, and tell him to wait a minute."

Her eyes got so big that I grinned and rephrased it. "Put him in the great room, if he'll go, and say I'll be right down if he doesn't mind waiting."

I went back upstairs and brushed at my hair and slipped on sandals, but that was it. No point in dolling up for some bald, uptight politician who wanted to complain about his daughter's living conditions and choice of friends. If he fussed too much, he could pack her up and take her away on the spot.

I tried to take the scowl off my face as I went down the front stairs, but it was still there as I stepped through the double doors into the great room.

Chapter 15

Tom Roddler wasn't uptight and, of course, he wasn't bald. I remembered about the hair as soon as I saw him. Except for the sideburns, now gone, and extra crinkles around the eyes, he looked pretty much like the picture on his mother's piano.

"Mrs. Shaw?"

"That's right." My eyes took in the sports shirt, khaki slacks and loafers, and returned to his face. He seemed positive to his mother's negative, amused blue eyes instead of faded brown ones, blonde hair instead of frost gray.

"I hope you don't mind me checking on Jerricha." His smile slipped briefly then came back full force. "It's a—kind of habit— and when my mother called, I thought I'd just run up and make sure she was okay."

I continued to study him from about ten feet away and

decided it was a family thing. Florence DeLong could be sixty-five as easily as eighty, Jerricha looked about half of her twenty-five years, and here, their genetic connection, was a guy who had to be in his sixties but could pass for forty-something after a couple of martinis. I shook myself mentally. Now that Alex was gone, I hoped my libido wasn't going to kick up every time somebody presentable appeared, especially somebody too old for me—never mind a politician.

Tom Roddler checked the watch on his right wrist. "I dropped Sherry downtown at headquarters." He stopped and clarified, "Sherry's my aide, and I've got an hour or so free. Any chance you'd have time for a drink or a cup of coffee? I'd like to talk to you about a couple of things."

I looked down at my shorts and T-shirt. "Have to be some place really casual."

"Not a problem." He waved goodbye to Jerricha, who was staring at the television and appeared not to notice, and led the way out the door.

A black Lexus was parked on the street next to the house, and he went around to open my door. Quite a difference from Alex, who always assumed I liked jumping in by myself.

Without any input from me, we drove straight to the Tiki Bar, a little place overlooking the Riverwalk, and I watched the man who wanted to be the next state senator charm the waitress into a small table reserved for people having dinner. When I ordered scotch and water, no ice, he smiled his approval.

"I have to say, you're not what I expected." He turned the blue eyes on me full strength. "And neither is your house."

"Your mother thinks we're a cult."

"I know. She asked me to, uh, speak to Jerricha."

"Did you?"

He nodded. "I told her the place looked all right but to watch herself. And not to drink the Kool Aid."

I grinned in spite of myself.

"Sorry if Florence was difficult. Jerricha's a big girl now, and she has to make her life work, but my mother doesn't see it that way. She's a product of her generation, a little rigid sometimes. Spent her life trying to do what was best for me." He rubbed a knuckle against his forehead. "And she got it wrong. Got married and moved to Oklahoma so I'd have a dad but she was an Eastern girl and she liked cities. She had no idea how remote it was going to be."

He glanced up at me and smiled. "I won't bore you with my dysfunctional childhood. And I'm not making excuses for Florence, it's just that she hasn't had an easy life, and she takes it out on Jerricha sometimes—and on Jerricha's friends."

At that moment, the drinks came, which gave me a chance to regroup. I like having my socks charmed off as much as the next potential voter, but my warning signals go off as soon as I hear the phrase, "I'm not making excuses." I heard it too many times during my nine-year marriage. It ranked right up there with "Trust me" and "I won't drink anything tonight."

Maybe that's why I took two or three good solid mouthfuls of scotch instead of sipping like I usually did. Or maybe I just didn't want him to be a disappointment.

He gave me an appraising look, opened his mouth to speak and closed it again. Then, "Jerricha said you were a college instructor. Were you always?"

I shook my head. "Just the last few years."

"And before?"

"Photojournalist."

"Yeah? Would I have seen any of your stuff?"

"I don't know. I interned in Toronto. After that I worked as a freelancer, and after that for Concepts magazine, late eighties, early nineties, mostly in Europe: London, France, Spain, Greece. It was a dream job, really."

"Must have been a culture shock when you moved to Seminole Beach."

"It was different."

"What made you quit?"

"Oh, I don't know." The scotch was starting to take hold, and I settled farther back in my chair. "It got more technological, and I liked the old ways—shooting pictures with fast black-and-white and a little grain for texture. The computerized stuff's too smooth. And the job got harder physically, wasn't as much fun as before. You get tired and wish you had a family to spend holidays with, stuff like that. My degree was in communications and I knew I could teach, so I got married and moved here. It seemed like the right thing."

"You still carry a camera around? So you don't miss the one picture nobody else will see?"

I shook my head. "Not anymore."

Not since the day my husband died, actually. No, ex-husband. The words seemed to hang in the air, although I hadn't said them aloud.

We were silent as the waitress delivered another round I hadn't seen him order.

"I did some traveling myself," he said when she'd gone, "quite a lot when I was younger. Walked most of the Appalachian Trail, sailed the Greek Islands, surfed off Ecuador. Took a train across India."

I finished the rest of my drink and started on the new one. "I love trains."

"You wouldn't have loved this one. It had boxcars you

shared with fifty other people and assorted animals, and you cooked your meals over an open fire."

"You made a fire in a boxcar?"

"We had these little burners." He grinned. "Wonder we didn't incinerate ourselves."

"Kind of a dream life too."

"Yeah, but I did what you did. Decided family mattered more." He eyed me over his glass. "You're very easy to talk to—unlike a lot of people. Could you stand two minutes of my life story if it were for a good cause?"

"Maybe." The scotch had warmed me through. "But I don't do sympathy votes."

He laughed out loud and tapped me lightly on the nose with his finger.

"I'd just like you to understand. My mother gets a little paranoid sometimes, particularly where Jerricha is concerned, but she was wrong about you. I promise it'll be the short version."

I studied him openly. He had it down pat: the body language, the eye contact, the flattering look, the suggestion that we shared something no one else appreciated. He was so good at it, I let it ride. "Go ahead."

"Okay. I met Jerricha's mother in college. She was a beautiful woman, but we were a million miles apart philosophically. We probably wouldn't have made it long term, but she died before it became an issue." He looked out at the river. "Jerricha was three at the time, and she's never really found her—spot—in life. That's a liability if your family's in the public eye."

I nodded. "Your mother said she was—that she had problems in school."

"She has attention deficit disorder, that's all." A trace of irritation showed in his face. "She's smart enough, but she doesn't remember information she hears, and that hurt her grades. Had a couple of bad teachers. She's young for her age; I'm sure you noticed that. And she believes anything she's told." He frowned. "Unless Florence or I are the ones telling her."

"Your mother seems kind of tough on her . . ."

"True, but we've been burned a number of times, and this death she seems to have stumbled across could be another problem. Last year she drove through a store window, did a lot of damage and lost her license. Before that she got picked up at some head-banger joint with a guy waving a gun around."

"Oh, well," I shrugged, "It happened to JLo, and she turned out all right."

"True." His frown shifted to a broad grin. "And I am boring you now."

"It's not that." I looked away from the blue eyes before they sucked me in and chewed me up. I'm a sucker for sexy eyes. "Look, I owed your daughter for backing me up with the police, and when she refused to go back to her friend Cindy's, I offered her a room. She's just filling in until our cook comes back." I crossed my arms over my chest and leaned back. "She hasn't been any trouble, and in spite of what your mother thinks, the people in the house are pretty straight. They're all Florida Art Grant recipients, and none of them does anything particularly weird or illegal or threatening. Her staying at the house isn't a problem, but if you really want me to, I'll boot her."

"Well, maybe you could just convince her she's better off where she was. My mother seems to feel pretty strongly about it." His eyes crinkled up. "Not me. I'd stick right there and figure I had it made." He paused and moved his glass around on the table. "Let me think about it. Okay if I call up every now and then to talk? See how she's doing?"

"So I can report on Jerricha's activities? That kind of thing?"

"Absolutely not." He reached out, took my hand in a warm,

firm grasp. "Unless she gets in trouble and needs real help, her name won't even come up. Okay?"

Our pulses were throbbing in perfect sync; I counted the beats. I nodded and eased my hand away. It was either that or drag him under the table and lay on top of him, which seemed a little pushy on such short acquaintance.

Chapter 16

From the journal, February 27, 1943
Afternoon

"We'll rest for a bit." The fair-haired man stepped back from the easel, his eyes still on the canvas. "Do you want to see?"

The girl pushed herself off the bar and took her time crossing the room. She circled the easel, not expecting very much, and came to a stop, astonished.

The woman in the painting actually looked like her: shiny dark hair just touching the shoulders, eyes long-lashed and seductive in a pale, oval face. The arms were especially elegant, smooth and bare. They flowed to ringless hands, nails painted red to match the floor-length dress.

The wall behind her was a swarm of pirates: pirates rowing ashore from a four-masted schooner, swinging on ropes, burying treasure in the sand. They were so full of color, so alive that she glanced at the wall behind the bar to make sure it was still plain, boring and cream colored.

After a moment, he spoke. "You say nothing. You don't like it."

"No," her eyes slid back to the woman in red. "I mean, yes, I love it. You're really good. Is this mine? To keep?"

"When it is finished." He turned and picked up a second canvas with a smile. "This one you may have now. A tiny masterpiece."

She took the small painting and stared at the naked body, her own, stretched out across the grand piano. Something shifted in her chest.

"You can see the woman is well loved." He nodded matter-of-factly. "Beautiful women have many pictures made of them. What is the song—from your Johnny Mercer? About being a beautiful baby?"

"Not me." Her laugh was edged with scorn. "I don't have any baby pictures."

"None at all?"

She laid the nude painting on the table. "Just a snapshot when I was three days old. My mother was holding me and staring out a window. There was snow on the ground, and she looked like a caged animal." She grinned at him "I don't have it anymore; I lost it."

He began to recap the tubes of oil paint. "Perhaps your mother did not like photographs."

She shrugged. "She took a lot when my sister was born. Dozens of little black-and-white snaps: first steps, first birthday, first tooth. Then we went to live with my aunt. No pictures after that."

He looked up with concern. "Your mother died?"

"No, she left us with Aunt Velda and went to California for some kind of job. She *said*."

"But you saw her again? Heard from her?"

"Yes and no. She sent train fare for my sister and said she'd send for me when she had the money saved up." She made a dismissive movement. "She never did."

"Perhaps she lost her job . . ."

"I don't think there was a job. She was living with some guy in San Diego. She sent a telegram once, when I was seven. Said the guy threw her out and she and my sister had nothing to eat. My aunt wired her twenty dollars, and that was the last we heard."

"Perhaps she felt you were better off—"

"Oh, right. She didn't care if my sister starved or lived on the street, she still wanted her there. But she didn't want me." She looked around the room. "Water under the bridge. Where are my cigarettes?"

In the silence, he picked up a piece of charcoal and began to sketch on a sheet of note paper.

The girl went to the bar, took a cigarette from a green tin box, lit it and watched him smudge in the charcoal with his fingers. "Now what are you doing?"

"Something occurred to me," he said without looking up.

She lifted her chin and blew smoke toward the ceiling. "Am I finished posing?"

"For today." He crossed the room and put the paper in her hand. "A gift for you."

He had used a minimum of charcoal lines and slashes, but she realized at once that it was a picture of her own seven-year-old face. The child's hair curled softly to its neck, the lips curved in a half smile, and the eyes, dark and thick-lashed, too young yet for defenses, looked straight into her own—trusting, a little sad, hoping to be loved.

The drawing blurred to white, and she jabbed out her cigarette in the ashtray, raised her chin and blinked her eyes. An old trick, a good trick, but this time it failed to work. Hot tears streaked down through her make-up onto her neck, as the seven-year-old began to sob, breaking its own heart. "I didn't lose it. I cut them in pieces, that woman and baby, in millions of pieces."

"It's all right, Florence, it's all right. She didn't mean—"

His words, appalled and meant to soothe, stopped the tears literally in their tracks. Her face turned white, and her eyes were ugly.

"Don't you dare stand up for that bitch. You don't know anything about it." She grabbed up her purse and cigarettes and headed for the door.

"Where are you going?"

"Out. I've been cooped up in this hellhole too damned long; it's making me screwy."

Chapter 17

When Bear pounded on my door the next morning, I'd had about four hours sleep, and jogging wasn't high on my priority list. Neither was raising my aching head a few inches off the pillow.

Tom Roddler, ignoring his own self-imposed time schedule, as well as that of his long-suffering aide, had driven me home just before midnight. We took the long way, cruising downtown and around Seminole Beach's prize landmark, a fountain with a bronze sailfish leaping into the air amidst ocean spray and skillful lighting. At night it reminded me of Paris without the traffic, and I loved it. Tom must have loved it too because we circled it three times, windows down to get the full effect of water flashing and splashing. After that we sat out in front of my house like teenagers with no place to go. Tom's aide must have been pacing the floor at Democratic headquarters.

I pretended not to hear Bear knocking and rolled over to face the wall, but a cynical Irish voice started sing-songing in my head: *Eat like a pig, drink like a pig, wake up a pig.* That was enough to get me out of bed, fully clothed, and downstairs. After that, it was all down hill.

On a good day, jogging is about as much fun as a cold water enema. When it's pre-dawn, already 80 degrees outside, and your fellow joggers choose to run on streets where the breeze is blocked by buildings and trees, it is less fun. We also had a little synchronization problem, since both Bear and Nita could jog for more than forty seconds at a time. Only Bear's desire to report on his investigation, which I'd already forgotten about, kept me from being left in the dust. As I struggled from block to block, he rattled on without a gasp for breath.

"I talked to Robbie Garcia's half brother, like you suggested."

Had I suggested that? "How'd you find him?" I panted, "his name wasn't in the paper."

"Phone book. There were eleven Garcias, and I punched numbers until I got somebody who knew Robert. An aunt or something. She said his half-brother's last name was Meir."

"Meir? She told you just like that?"

"I was charming and persuasive," he said, smirking. "I looked up the address and went out to the house. Said I owed him some money, and his wife told me where he worked."

"And?"

"He flipped out. The minute he heard Robbie's name, he started yelling. According to him, the kid was a dead loss from age fourteen. Dropped out of school, did crap jobs or no jobs, dragged the family from one mess to another. The parents spent money they didn't have on speech therapists, because nobody could understand him, and blew their savings on child psychologists. But the guy really went berserk when I asked about their sister. Said she made Robbie worse and told me to get the hell out."

"So," I was puffing harder, "waste of time then. Nobody liked Robbie except his half sister, and she's a bad ass too."

Bear punished me by picking up speed. "Then I went down to look at the Trimaran."

"Yeah, why?" I came to a complete stop under a street light, partly in surprise and partly because I had to rest or die. Bear and Nita stopped too but continued to jog in place.

"Because," Bear said, overly patient, "You saw a ripple off the bow."

"Oh, yeah. Probably just a mullet jumping."

"Maybe. I took the kayak out and went aboard to have a look."

"Really? Hopefully nobody saw you and called the owner."

"It was dark, and the guy's in Switzerland. They can't even find him to make him move it. Anyway, somebody had snapped the lock on the transom and then rigged it back so it looked locked up. I jiggled it around and went below, and guess what I found?"

"Cocaine cookies?"

"Uh-uh. Smelly blankets and a bunch of empty beer and Vienna sausage cans. Half a loaf of stale bread and a lot of roaches."

"Ugh." That was the first sound I'd heard from Nita.

"And I started thinking it'd be damned easy to swim from the Tri to the end of the boat dock without being seen. And when Robbie came up in the rowboat, he shot up out of the water, and—*Wham!*"

Nita stopped jogging. "You think somebody stabbed Robbie and swam back to the boat to hide out?"

112   *False Impression*

Bear nodded his head at her. "Why not? Jerricha wouldn't have noticed—in spite of what she says."

"The police must have searched the boat," I objected, "They'd find the guy."

"I doubt it." Bear was wearing gold sweat pants cut just above the knee and a hooded, orange sweatshirt left open to frame a bare, tanned chest and tight abs. He looked and sounded like a leftover from *Miami Vice*. "Lock's rusted, and unless you played with it, you'd think it was in place. Cops don't break into locked boats without permission."

"Unlike some of us," I muttered.

He ignored me. "Anyway, I figure the guy didn't wait 'til the police came, just got his stuff and went back in the water. When Jerricha ran off to find a phone and you were talking to the fisherman, he swam to the bank on your blind side. Or waded, maybe, it's pretty shallow in there."

"And then what? Walked down the street soaking wet and hoped nobody saw him?"

Bear finally stopped running in place. "Nope, changed clothes, got on his bike and showed up in the park a few minutes later to ask you and Louie the fisherman what was going on."

My eyes opened wide for the first time that morning. Everywhere I turned the kid with the web tattoo and the ass-revealing pants showed up. Not that I thought Bear was right.

"What happened to your theory that Jerricha saw somebody she knew kill him and kept quiet about it?" I said maliciously.

"Early days yet." Bear leaned down to tie his shoe, "C'mon, only three miles to go."

I shook my head. "This is it for me. I'm not feeling too good."

"Too much to drink last night with Jerricha's father?"

I gave him a look. "How'd you know about that?"

"She said that's where you went, and my window was open when he dropped you off." He didn't exactly leer, but it was close.

"Yeah, well, I'd keep that window closed if I were you, considering how much I just paid for the air conditioning. I'm heading back."

"Wait, two more things," Bear dropped into a lunge to stretch the back of his leg. "One, Jerricha got a threatening phone call yesterday. She says it was a wrong number, but Jesse heard her end and said she was scared. She won't answer the kitchen phone now, just lets it ring."

"Any idea who?"

"Nope. The second thing is even more curious: Jerricha's father was in Seminole Beach Sunday morning, the day the kid got his lunch down on the dock."

"What? How do you know that?"

"I was up at four this morning and went to get a paper. He had a breakfast meeting with the county's Democratic Party chairman. Didn't he mention it? He's all over the local section."

"Are you suggesting that Tom Rodd—"

"Not suggesting anything. Nita! C'mon, let's move."

Nita sketched a wave at me, and I watched them jog down the street. Obviously, Bear investigating was going to be a whole lot worse than Bear sitting naked in the bathtub typing up theories.

I walked slowly back to the house. It was humid and dark out, and there were nasty little noises, things scrabbling out of sight, things rustling in the bushes. You don't notice sounds like that unless you're alone. I avoided the hedge-lined sidewalks and walked in the middle of the car-lined street.

"What're you doing out this early?"

The man's voice was gruff and very close to my right shoulder. I jumped about a foot and turned to look at a nearby pickup truck. The driver's window was down, but it was too dark to see a face on the dark body sitting there. For a second I didn't move, then I ran like hell for the back door of our house. When I got there, I fumbled away precious seconds getting the key out of my pocket before realizing the door was unlocked. I slammed it shut behind me and turned the dead bolt.

By the time I calmed down and got my breath back, I felt like an idiot. Why was I so afraid of a freaking voice? It was probably just some guy who'd overdosed on six packs and was sleeping it off in his own vehicle. Practically a Seminole Beach sport. It wasn't until I got upstairs that I realized it might have been Alec's truck. But if it was Alec, why was he sitting out in front of his own house at five o'clock on a Saturday morning?

Three hours later I was clean, dressed and on my way to Park Place to see Eileen Coates or Ellen Cortez or whatever combination of names worked.

Once I had made the decision to locate her, I was aware that calling ahead was the correct thing to do. Unfortunately, healthcare directors, like bureaucrats, get paid to think up ways to thwart the general public, and being thwarted isn't good for anyone's self-esteem. Better to show up, say I was writing a book and throw myself on the mercy of the receptionist. The worst she could say was nothing doing. I did wear a jeans skirt instead of shorts to fool her into thinking I was appropriately dressed.

The reception room at Park Place had groups of mauvy-pink sofas flanked by small, mahogany tables, and all of its magazines were up-to-date. The woman at the desk was pale, about thirty and very helpful.

"I'll check with the director, "she said, when I told her I'd like to see Mrs. Coates, "but I'm sure it'll be all right. Eileen loves having company." She lowered her voice a little, tone confidential. "It's her craft time right now, but she doesn't really like it. She just rolls her eyes when they take out the glue and scissors."

I smiled as she left the desk. She'd handed me the woman's first name on a platter and my first, albeit mumbled, guess on the last name had been an instant winner. The day was beginning to improve.

A few minutes later, I was perched on a folding chair next to a woman in a brown Barcalounger. She was pushed back into reclining position, her walker within easy reach.

Eileen Coates had limp, grayish-brown hair, thin on top, and no expression at all. I introduced myself and leaned close in case she was hard of hearing.

"I wanted to ask you some questions about the Forties. Do you remember World War II? What you were doing then?" I took a notebook out of my purse and waited.

Her head turned slightly toward me, but she didn't respond.

Another elderly woman with dyed, black hair edged up to my chair. She was holding a picture frame made of clothespins. "I know about it. My husband was at D-Day. But he didn't like the movie."

"Go away. She came to see me!" Mrs. Coates struggled upright. "Pull that thing so I can sit up," she muttered, looking down at the adjustment bar. The black-haired woman wandered away.

Mrs. Coates settled back and blinked at me. "Now, what did you say?"

Her voice was definitely the one on the missing recorder.

"Um, I think you had a visitor a while ago, a young man

with dark hair who talked to you about the Forties, right?"

After a moment, she nodded. "Oh, him. He did. A lot of questions."

"And you told him about the spies who were here."

"Spies? The rich ones?"

"I'm not sure. They were here during the war, I think."

"It's hard to remember—a long time ago."

"I know, but you told him about some people in town who took food and gas out to the submarines?"

"Gas?" Silence. Then, "He had an X sticker you know, not many people did, and he could go anywhere he wanted, any time. He had a Packard too. Not brand new, they didn't make new cars during the war, but it was a nice, black one. And that fancy Buccaneer."

"Buccaneer?"

"Clyde loved that boat, always a lot of people having a good time. A lot of girls came to stay, service wives. Here one day, gone the next."

"Clyde was your husband?"

"Yes. No. He died. He drowned." She closed her eyes. "I don't talk about that. They got the other one out, though, and I don't think anybody ever knew. They thought they both died." Her eyes opened suddenly. "Well, he did . . . but not like they thought. Terrible thing about Rennie. He hated being locked up, so he died too."

"Who died, Mrs. Coates?"

"The handsome one . . ." Her eyes closed again. "I'm tired."

"Of course. I just wondered."

She rolled her head from side to side on the back of the chair. "Not Rennie, it was the other one. The one that was crazy about her. He called me Lena, you know, not Eileen. But Rennie paid for everything. Of course he would be crazy about her. None of the other girls had clothes like that. Big-city clothes."

"I—" I began.

"He painted her in those fancy clothes sometimes, other times, well," she made a noise like a giggle, "not so many. Once on the piano. He played it too, not boogie-woogie, though. She'd sit there and listen to him for hours. Longest she ever sat still. I never saw anybody cared more about how they looked. Hours, she spent. It was a beautiful house, all those arches and picnics by the river. Rennie could get anything: sugar, coffee, cream, chocolate, even in rationing. She didn't appreciate it, though. Lazy as sin; thought anything she wanted should just pop out of the lamp. He wasn't Rennie, though. He didn't do everything she wanted." She leaned back in the chair. "I'm too tired now. You can go."

"Okay." I stopped taking notes and sat still. "Thanks for talking to me."

"Did she send you?"

"Who?"

"I said, 'Don't send me here. I hate it here. Jailers.' " Her head went back and forth on the pillow. "Watchin' to see where I put things. I used to go to the other place—you know, the Cunsal. No, that's not right. I didn't sleep there, nobody did, but the food was good. And we danced. The chicken song, the YMCA. At the cuncil, concil . . ."

"You don't mean the Council on Aging?"

"Yes." Her face lightened for a second. "I liked that. I could have stayed in my house. I hate this place." She slid her eyes sideways at me. "Will you take me there? You can go if some-body takes you, but that boy's not good for anything. Does what she says, and they won't let me drive anymore. I could always drive a lot better than her."

118   *False Impression*

From the look of her right arm and the side of her face, I was pretty sure she'd had a stroke. I took the gutless way out. "I'll see what I can do."

Her eyes struggled to focus on me. "If you take me there, I'll tell you all about it. Here!" Her left hand went into the pocket of her sweater and pulled out a closed fist. "You keep this. You keep this for me."

"But . . ."

"It's Clyde's. They tried to take it away, but I hid it. You give it to me when you come back. She pressed something hard into my hand. "Hide it. Hurry, you can't trust any of them. You give it to me when you come back."

"All right, Mrs. Coates." I shoved the object in my skirt pocket without looking at it and waited a few minutes, but she'd either gone to sleep or she was doing an excellent imitation.

On the way out, the cheerful receptionist called to me. "How was your visit?"

"She seems a little tired," I said. "Does her family come by to see her?"

The woman shook her head. "I don't think she has any children, and her husband died a year or so ago."

"Oh. I thought she said he drowned during the war."

"Oh, no, he was ninety. He was here with us too." She smiled at me. "They get confused, you know, about time. Years don't mean much when you live nearly a hundred of them."

"I guess not. So nobody visits her? No sisters or brothers?"

"No family that I know of. Just a man who comes by every once in a while and brings a package for her. He may be a great nephew or something."

I nodded. That must have been Joey, getting her on tape.

"He's an interesting guy," she went on, "has a very funny tattoo on his hand, like a web."

I stared at her. "A web?"

She smiled. "Isn't that odd? So many young people seem to have tattoos these days."

"Yes." I smiled back, but my brain was doing a flip. "It's very nice here," I said casually. "Can you get some kind of assistance if you're on a limited income?"

The woman shook her head with what looked like genuine regret. "We don't take Medicare. Which reminds me, do you have releases to sign? For the article you're doing?"

I looked at her blankly before I remembered the cover story. "Oh, no, I won't be using names or exact conversations."

"Just gathering background?"

"Right." I thanked her and went out to the car and unlocked the door. Eileen Coates didn't seem to have any money, so if she also had no children or relatives, who was the *she* who paid for her to live in an expensive facility like Park Place? And wasn't it a huge coincidence that Web Boy visited her regularly?

I drove back over the causeway trying to think, but my head wasn't helping. I needed a large cup of coffee in the worst way. Time to swear off scotch and stick to wine.

I was so intent on a caffeine fix, I had pulled up in front of Spike O's before I remembered the object in my skirt pocket. I'd meant to leave it at the front desk.

It looked like a Celtic cross of some kind, a drab bronze medal with a faded black-and-white ribbon. I held it up in the light and the medal twisted around.

Not a cross after all. Not with that swastika etched on one side.

Chapter 18

From the journal, February 27, 1943
Midnight

No lights were allowed within ten miles of the shore now, not even in the small towns.

The couple slipped out the side door of the Arcade and moved cautiously down the sloping yard to the river. Behind them, the blackout lamps faded to nothing, "In the Mood" bounced to its jazzy finish, and somebody dropped another nickel in the juke box. "String of Pearls" floated out through the screened windows.

"Oh—sand burrs!" The girl came to a halt in ankle-high grass. "And this is the last pair of silk hose I have."

"Never mind." PFC Grimes lifted her off the ground and

swung her out across the expanse of weeds and rocks and sugar sand. He set her down, giggling and out of breath, on a tiny strip of smooth, pale beach.

There was no moon, and it was too dark at first to separate black river from black sky. She felt the movement of water, heard the steady waves rolling in, lapping out the sounds of Glenn Miller, but her eyes were slow to adjust.

His face, an oblong blur, hovered above her. "Don't move. I'll be back in a minute."

"What . . . ?"

"I'm getting us something better than coffee to drink, but I want you where the other guys can't carry you off."

"The bugs may carry me off."

"Not tonight. Too much wind." He handed her a palm frond. "Here, brush 'em off like a real Floridian. But don't move!" He loped off through the weeds, a tall, khaki shadow.

She gave the frond a tentative pass around her head and waited, listening for the high-pitched whine of mosquitoes. One minute, and that was it. Sixty seconds flat or back to the dance, sand burrs or not.

A large, powerful hand shot out of the darkness and grasped her arm just above the elbow. "Don't scream. Get in the boat."

For a second she couldn't move.

"I have a date." It came out in a whisper as her breath returned. "He'll be back any second."

"A boy." The voice was low. "You deserve much better than a boy."

"Let go!" She jerked her arm, but he kept it without effort.

"We go for a ride. Get in the boat."

"I'm busy."

"Not as busy as you soon will be."

His right hand slipped from her arm to her waist and tightened.

His left came up with a clicking sound, and a small circle of light flashed on a cryptic face and pale-blonde hair.

"Put that out." Her voice was sharp. "What if somebody sees you?"

"If you get in the boat, they won't." Light-blue eyes, amused and impatient, looked into hers. "You knew it was me?"

She didn't answer.

"You are still angry."

"Damn straight. You have a lot of nerve, mister, following me here."

He clicked off the flashlight. "How could I follow? You came with Rennie in the Packard. I was fishing and saw the lights of the dance. Imagine my surprise to find you beside the river."

"I'm having a good time, and I'm going back in." Her voice was hard.

"No. Ordinarily I would allow it, but time is short, and I do not propose to waste it."

"Your problem." She struggled to get loose.

"True." He made a bored sound, dropped her arm and stepped away. "There are undoubtedly things of more interest. Here, for instance—such waste." His voice cooled as his attention shifted away from her. "All this land and no one makes it beautiful. They should build a dock and a walkway all along the water. And a musik kapellenstand—what do you call it—for a band? So one could walk and dance in moonlight over the top of the water. A river walk and a river dance. You know?"

"Engineer talk."

"Not so much." He turned to look at her. "You will get in the boat. And you will come back with me and be divested of your shoes and the silk hose you told the boy about. And all the rest. Or we can do that here, and he will have a surprise when he returns."

"You wouldn't dare." Her voice wavered, and she controlled it. "Anyway, you're crazy to be out. They're patrolling tonight—two fishing trawlers—watching for suspicious boats."

"There are three, actually. One is just by the channel marker." He reached out and slowly ran a thumb from her earlobe down to the space between her breasts. "They were drinking whiskey, and I used the oars. No one knew I was there. Don't be angry anymore. Get in the boat."

The open skiff slid noiselessly out into the water, seconds before PFC Grimes called from the shore.

"I got a pint of . . . Hey! Where'd you go?

Chapter 19

Spike O's was nearly empty; it was too late for the breakfast crowd and too early for lunch. I sipped at a plain, black roast, relaxed in the silence, and opened the paper. Bear was right; Tom Roddler was all over it. There was only one paragraph about his 9:00 a.m. Sunday breakfast meeting in Seminole Beach, but there was a half page spread of him dedicating a plaque to World War II servicemen two days earlier in Miami.

He took a good picture, handsome and boyish in a dark suit and red power tie. He called the men who trained at Officer Candidate School "the ultimate heroes, twenty-year-olds who saw a job that needed doing and did their best to get it done," and claimed Brokaw's book, *The Greatest Generation*, should be mandatory reading in every high school in the country. He also mentioned that today's teens were "historically illiterate."

That was safe enough; none of them were old enough to vote.

The reporter had included a couple of paragraphs about Tom's father and stepfather. Those wouldn't do his campaign one bit of harm; both men were heroes, one decorated at Anzio, the other awarded a posthumous Purple Heart. There were little oval pictures of Lt. Frank Roddler, dark haired and eyed, and Herbert DeLong, blonde and solid looking. Tom looked a lot more like his step dad than his real one.

"Freedom isn't cheap," he said in a half-inch quote, "and we have more of it than any country in the world. We have it because my fathers, like thousands of others, were willing to pay the price."

I took in a deep breath. Louie Janclowski was right; nowhere did Tom mention global warming or the Taliban or the tanked housing industry. Did he plan to do it all on patriotism? Didn't he know he was a Democrat?

On the opposite page there was a follow-up story about Florence DeLong's former twenties mansion. The Michigan couple who purchased the house had decided to build something gigantic and pink on the property and sell off the existing buildings. The house and adjacent garage would be floated down the river to somebody's private island. A picture of a bulldozer sitting in the front yard complemented the article.

I folded up the papers, got a refill for the road and went home. No pickup trucks, including Alec's, were parked on either side of our street at the moment.

Jerricha was in the kitchen stirring a giant pot of something bubbly and thick on Amy's stove. I offered her the newspaper article, but she wasn't interested.

"I know all about it. My dad called this morning, and the house thing is a big mess. Grandmother's really mad they're moving it. She called up the people and wanted to buy it back, but they won't sell." She pushed a handful of hair behind one ear and struck a pose, hand on one hip, platform sandal extended. "I think he was really just calling for you."

"Oh, yeah?"

"Well, he wanted to know when you'd be home and said he might call back this evening."

"Okay." I hooked two slices of ham out of the refrigerator and rolled each around a dill pickle.

"Women are always hanging all over him, especially Sherry, his personal assistant." The words *Sherry* and *personal* dripped acid. "He does stuff they like."

I ate one of the ham rolls. "Like what?"

"Oh, you know." She stared into the cooking pot. "He tells them he used to surf in South America somewhere and went to Indiana to backpack and learn Hyundai."

"You mean India? Hindu?"

"Whatever." She said flatly. "I mean, he'll never marry any of them. Why should he? The one at his house is rich too, really rich. Sherry isn't, but he'll keep her around as long as she's useful." She shook her head. "If he tells you you're the only one he can really talk to, he's just saying it. He tells them all the same thing."

"Really?" I eyed her thoughtfully. "Did you actually answer the phone when he called? I hear we've been getting weird calls lately."

The spoon she was holding hit the side of the pan and slipped out of her hand and into the red, sticky mess.

"See what you made me do!" Her voice was furious.

"Sorry, but—"

"I don't know anything about it." She turned her back on me and kept it there until I gave up and went upstairs.

Tom Roddler didn't call back that night, not that I waited around for him. But when the phone rang at 7:40 the next morning, I half expected to hear his voice. Instead it was Ben.

"Just called to say I'm back in town. Have you seen the Sentinel? They're going to fill it in any minute, and we'll want pictures. You'll have to get out there today."

I yawned and tossed my pen on the kitchen table. "You lost me, Benjamin. I haven't seen or heard anything this morning. I've been working on your project for the last hour: the incomparable highlights of nineteen forty-four."

"Great, fine, but you need to check out the DeLong house. They found a basement under it when they put it up on rollers yesterday. They think it was used for smuggling rum. It's got a tunnel running down to the river, and the reporter swears he saw eight-foot pirates painted on the walls . . ."

"There aren't any basements in Florida, and they smuggled rum in the twenties, not the Forties."

"There certainly are basements here. They'll put one in if you want it, but they're too expensive to bother with. Anyway, I was about to say, before I was so rudely interrupted, there are also German U-boats painted all over, an entire wall of them."

"So? U-boats were a big deal in Florida during World War II. Anybody could have painted them for any reason at all—and at any time."

"Maybe, but they kept the ship sinkings very quiet in the early Forties so the rest of the country wouldn't panic. And it worked; in Chicago they didn't even know there was a war on. This could be a great find, an incredible addition to the video."

"Hold on, hold on. You said to give you fourteen minutes of filler and it didn't even have to be good."

"I know what I said," Ben's voice was testy, "but let's not roll over dead on this, Keegan. Florida During Wartime could be seen all over the country. You need to get out there with a camera."

"That wasn't part of the deal. You know I don't do that anymore. Anyway, the reporter must have gotten pictures."

"Just the house sitting up on rollers. The rest weren't clear."

"And you expect me to do better? If there are wall paintings, and they're any age at all, they'll be faded and moldy."

"What about that Japanese guy you've got living with you? The photography whiz? Didn't he restore a lot of old photos for some museum?"

"Well, yeah, but Kenji's busy, and he doesn't work free."

"Just get him out there. I'll find some money somewhere. I have to go. Call me later."

"Wait, Ben, the new owners aren't going to like us poking around."

"They're back in Michigan—read your morning paper. There's only a moving crew out there and some guy with a bulldozer who says he's going to lay a slab right over the whole basement, which means filling it in. Oh, and by the way, when the reporter called Florence DeLong for a quote, she said the house never had a basement."

I opened my mouth to comment, but he'd already hung up.

There's only one way to handle Ben when he's on a tear: Do what he wants and get it over with. I sat still for maybe ten seconds, then shoved some money in my pocket, pocketed my car keys and went up to Kenji's room. When he opened his door, colored lights flashed off the walls behind him.

"Hello, Keegan. What goes on?"

"I need you to get your best camera and take pictures of a basement full of pirates. Now, if you can."

There's never any point in getting into long discussions with

Kenji; he either will do something or he won't, and he decides on the spot.

He was looking down at the floor as he translated. "Pirates?"

"Right."

"One moment." He closed the door.

Now, what does that mean? I raised my hand to knock again. "You'll get paid." I called louder. "And I'll buy you coffee."

The door opened, and he came out wearing baggy surfer shorts, a wrinkled, black tee shirt and sandals. He carried two cameras by their straps. One had a telescopic lens that was almost obscene.

I stopped by Spike O's for two extra-large coffees, and Kenji and I soaked up caffeine all the way to Florence DeLong's house—now literally once removed. As I turned off Palm Beach Road onto a graveled driveway, Kenji pointed out a piece of cardboard propped against one of the ornate gate posts. KEEP OUT!!!!! had been scrawled in red felt-tip letters.

I eyed the exclamation marks. "The owners aren't here, and there's just a crew working. Why bother warning people away?"

"Maybe people come in crowds to look. Paper says of historical significance," he slurred the word a little, "so history people want to see."

"Damn, I forgot to pick up a paper."

"Have mine when we return."

I smiled to myself. Obviously, he'd read all about the basement, which was why he agreed to come. I could have saved Ben money if I'd remembered how much Kenji loved gossip and how he considered American history merely a sanitized extension of it. Current events or a hundred years ago, Thomas Jefferson or back-biting on American Idol, it was all the same to him.

I parked the car a little down the winding lane, and we got out. You could see the Mizner house sitting on wheels down by the river. There was a large, gaping hole in the middle of the property, and the entire yard—trees, grass and bushes—had been bulldozed into four giant piles. The once-beautiful waterfront site was now a large plot of bare, yellow-brown earth scarred with tractor treads. Only the garage with its servants' quarters and the huge banyan tree remained intact.

As we navigated uneven piles of dirt and good-sized rocks, a short, stocky guy with clubbed hair and sleepy eyes stepped out from behind a dump truck and raised a hand.

"You need something?" he said with a half smile.

"I'm supposed to get pictures of the basement under Mrs. DeLong's house." I gestured at Kenji's cameras.

He looked me in the face, eyes half open. "You a reporter or something?"

"Uh, no. Doing a video for the history department at the college. They think the walls have historical significance."

"Well, maybe," he folded his arms and shook his head, "but the guys are pretty tied up right now clearing the area, and it's not safe down there. I'm supposed to tell people to wait up 'til the house is moving down river, then to take a look. You understand, right?"

"We would be very careful," Kenji spoke up, shifting the cameras to his other arm.

"Yeah, sure, but I can't let you take a chance. My job, you know?"

His body language said he'd made up his mind and wouldn't be changing it soon. I pointed at a guy bulldozing up a huge pile of dirt. "He's not going to fill the basement in today is he?"

"No ma'am. Not for a week or two, at least. Lot to do down there."

"Okay, thanks."

Kenji and I turned and headed back to the car.

As we drove back down the gravel road, past the Keep Out sign, Kenji spoke.

"Not workman, I think."

"Why not?"

"Sandals." He looked down at his own Birkenstocks. "Construction guys wear boots."

"Maybe they hired him to stand there and turn people away."

"Maybe he hides and workmen don't know. This picture is necessary?"

I took a right onto Palm Beach Road. "Well, yeah."

"Then we take when he is gone."

"What if he stands there all day?"

"Then maybe Bear takes ride on boat tonight, and we go too."

I could feel the grin spread slowly across my face. "You mean, sneak out here from the river side? It's hard enough getting decent shots in daylight. How do we get pictures in the dark?"

"No problem." Kenji looked pleased. "Have camera for that."

Bear didn't have a boat, really, he just had the use of one. And it belonged to his friend, and my former close friend and neighbor, Alec Pace. I wouldn't have asked Alec for anything, but Bear didn't seem to have a problem with it. He told Kenji he'd have the boat ready to go at ten p.m.

That resolved, I sat down to read Kenji's newspaper. The reporter, sounding excited, insisted he'd seen the outlines of a two-masted schooner and pirates swinging on ropes, as well as the faint outline of submarines. He said the new house was going to be built in the same space the old house had occupied, and the basement would be filled in as soon as possible for safety's sake. If that were true, the guy with sleepy eyes had lied. So, was he trying to rid himself of rubberneckers or just a loony with too much time on his hands?

Speaking of loonies, which Florida has more of, per capita, than any state in the union, there was a message from Florence DeLong on my answering machine upstairs. She had changed her mind and "would be happy to be interviewed for the college's video project on the war." She was now living at a new development called Little Clam Bay, she said, and would be free the next morning at 10:30, if that was convenient for me. She looked forward to being a contributor..

That didn't sound like the Mrs. DeLong I'd met a week ago, but I wasn't going to argue. Still, I wondered how helpful she'd be if she knew we were going to explore her former basement—the one she said wasn't there—as soon as it got dark.

Chapter 20

Bear cut the engine and reached for the emergency oar.
"Better keep the noise down so the neighbors don't call the police," he murmured and steered the boat silently toward the bank.

In the dark, sitting up on giant, wheeled dollies, Mrs. De-Long's prized Mizner house hovered over the river like a deformed dinosaur. Moonlight touched its arches and empty Palladian windows and silvered the hydraulics machinery that would load it onto a barge. A few feet below it, a row of mangroves clung to the riverbank on either side of a wooden seawall shored with creosote posts.

Bear let the Boston Whaler drift silently between mangroves and seawall until it nosed up to the bank. Then he and Kenji stepped out into shallow water. I slid out of my

133

Topsiders and into a pair of flip-flops, grabbed the flashlight and followed.

As he pulled the hull up on solid ground, Bear spoke in a raspy voice. "I better stick with the boat in case we need to move out in a hurry."

He was wearing a T-shirt that read: I KILLED A SIX PACK JUST TO WATCH IT DIE, and his eyes were brighter than the time he fell for the seventeen-year-old with a baby named Genesis and an older-man habit. He'd obviously reached a crossroads in his writing career and was moving permanently away from bunnies.

Kenji shifted the camera straps around his neck and started up the graded slope to the right of the property. I waded out of the warm water and tagged along. Dirt slid into my flip-flops and turned instantly to mud, but Kenji was still wearing the Birkenstocks, and if he could take it so could I. Just so we didn't step in a fire ant hill.

The ground was uneven, and it seemed like a long time before the slope leveled off. When the moon slid behind a bank of clouds and stayed there, we slowed down, feeling our way toward where the house had been. I was now in the lead, taking my bearings from the garage and servant's quarters, but in the dark I misjudged the distance. We got there sooner than I expected and nearly went face first into the pit that Mrs. DeLong insisted was not a basement. Kenji grabbed my arm and held on as I stumbled, and we both ended up on the ground.

The dozen or so homes on Sunrise Point had been built on full-acre lots, so the nearest ones were a healthy distance away. But we hadn't fallen quietly, and the moon, out again now, lit up the bare dirt yard, making sitting ducks out of us, or rather laying ones.

"What are you doing?" I hissed the words impatiently.

"Lens must stay open for few minutes. Light is ready?"

"Yeah," I held up the powerful torch. "But maybe we should wait. Maybe tomorrow . . ."

"Somebody watches house all day, and road is chained and locked at dusk." His voice came back low and farther away. "Hold, um, my feet."

He slid forward on his stomach and stretched out over the black hole in front of us, arms and head disappearing into the dark. I sat obediently on the back of his legs as he edged even farther forward, pointing the camera.

"Okay, put on light."

I clicked the switch and pointed the torch down.

"To right," his disembodied voice ordered.

I shifted the beam, and a flash went off accompanied by a series of soft clicks.

The moonlight illuminated little of the basement. You could see four walls crumbling at the top where the house had been pulled loose, but that was about it. If there were paintings, I couldn't see them.

For the next few minutes I concentrated on holding the torch steady on each of the walls, but I felt an impatience I hadn't experienced for a long time. I should have been the one taking the pictures. I had never lost my touch, just my desire to record the journey.

"Nearly done." Kenji's whisper floated up to me, and I let out a breath of relief.

Three seconds later his cell phone went off.

"Shit, shit, shit." Somebody kept saying. It was me.

"Hey! Who the hell's there?"

The voice sounded so violent, so jarring in that silent field, that I almost lost Kenji down the hole. I grabbed his legs and flattened down, scanning the site, trying to locate the speaker.

As Kenji's cell phone finished playing *The Godfather* theme, I heard thudding feet and a flashlight slashed across the ground on the other side of the pit.

"Who's there? Who the fuck's over there?"

It didn't sound like the guy who stopped us that morning, but when you're having a heart attack it's sometimes difficult to distinguish voices.

"One minute," Kenji's hoarse whisper came to me from down below. "One . . . minute. Keep light steady." Flash, *click*, *click*, *click*. Flash, *click*, *click*, *click*.

"Hey! You there! "The beam of light fastened on my face. "Get outta there! Get the fuck outta there!"

My first reaction, to shut my eyes, wasn't brilliant. I was trying to think of a second reaction when there was a scuffling sound and the light slid off my face. I stopped holding my breath and shook Kenji's leg.

"Come *on*," I ordered and was interrupted by a terrific *boom* as something *whooshed* over our heads.

I dropped the torch and tugged on Kenji's legs, but he didn't need any encouragement. He came out of the hole like toothpaste out of a new tube, bounced to his feet and raced me neck and neck across the cleared field toward the river.

Moving that fast was significantly different from picking your way. I hit a cluster of earthy clods, kept running, hit a pile of something bigger and harder, stumbled and ended up on my face. There was a second *boom* behind us and more yelling. Now there were two voices along with the sound of thudding feet.

Kenji darted back, grabbed my wrist and jerked me to my feet. "Must hurry."

"No shit." I was already out of breath, and we were still fifty yards from the river. I quit trying to breathe at all and concentrated on running longer than my record forty seconds. As we tore down the slope, I heard the engine catch on a boat and hoped it was our boat and Bear was the one catching it.

"Get in! Get in!" Bear was calling from offshore. He'd moved the Whaler back off the bank, and Kenji and I had to splash through water up to our waist to reach it. Bear reached out a muscled arm and dragged us into the boat one after the other.

"You see 'em?" a voice shouted. There were at least two of them, and they had reached the riverbank. "You see where they went? Gimme back the gun, man. Put the light on 'em. Where's the light?"

"Wait, you asshole. Somebody probably called the cops already."

As the boat reached deeper water, Bear let out the throttle and shot backwards away from shore, steering out into the wide river. The light of a strong torch flashed through the water where we'd been, but there was no accompanying *boom*. I held my breath as we put another hundred yards between us and the row of mangroves, then the whaler turned and roared in the opposite direction, spewing out a glittering, white-silver wake in the moonlight.

I leaned into the bow and let the waves splash my face as we ran full-out. I was cold, soaking wet, short one pair of flip-flops and a flashlight, and had probably pulled a shoulder socket getting aboard, but I had a huge grin on my face. There's nothing like the rush of almost being caught.

"You guys all right?" Bear shouted from the stern.

"Did you get the pictures?" I shouted at Kenji, who was crouched over the centerboard, doing something to his camera.

He raised his head and nodded. "Two rolls. Cost extra now."

"Okay." I had no desire to argue. "What, hazard pay? You lose a lens?"

"Neither." He held one foot up in the air. "Birkenstocks ruined."

Chapter 21

From the journal, March 6, 1943

The Packard clung to the edge of the black strip of highway, slowing from forty-five to twenty, then to a crawl. Flashes of lightning illuminated scruffy hedgerows and trees, eventually backlighting a rutted dirt trail that veered off the road to the left. The driver stopped the car, turned on the dome light for a few seconds and consulted a scrap of paper. Then he eased the vehicle onto the trail and jolted along under ficus trees that had grown together to form a canopy. Ground fog hovered a foot high, nearly obscuring the faded sign identifying Alton Groves.

"Couldn't you pick a better place than this?" the girl complained. "Some place a little less spooky?"

For once Rennie didn't laugh. "Not my fault. They just told me where he'd be. He chose the spot."

"How could he possibly know where to go?"

"They picked oranges here for two months." He broke off as the car rattled and shuddered its way along the washboard road, then resumed in an irritated voice. "He was sure he could find the bridge."

"Should we go this far off the main road? What if they're out looking for him? A posse or a patrol or something? What if they trap us in here?"

"Nobody goes looking for them." Rennie turned off the headlights and switched to fog lights. Diffuse, yellow light spread out in a haze before them. "At least not for forty-eight hours. The guards say they're happy to come back after a few days of swamp life. The last guy who escaped hung himself from a tree by the side of the road."

The girl shuddered.

"Okay." The car crept over an old, humpback bridge and along another thirty feet. "Should be about here, the third cattle gate on the other side." Rennie shifted into neutral and set the hand brake. "You stay here." He reached over the back seat for two of the mosquito sacks. "Keep the windows closed, or you'll be sorry." He pulled one piece of netting over his head and tied it around his waist with a cotton string. Then he grabbed the other piece, threw open the car door and lurched out.

The door slammed shut almost immediately but not soon enough. The car instantly filled with the low-pitched whine of mosquitoes. The girl reached in back for the third piece of netting and edged it over her head and shoulders. Then she pulled her feet up under her skirt and huddled on the seat.

Rennie stood in front of the car, feet disappearing into the fog, and waited. The mosquito netting made him a fantastic figure in the thin, sulfurous light.

There was nothing out here, no houses, no people, no vehicles. Just miles of snake and bug infested wilderness. A jagged flash of light lit the sky above the canopy of trees, and seconds later an earsplitting crash of thunder set the car windows rattling. The boom shook the girl too, and afterward she could no longer see Rennie in the headlights.

Just when she decided they'd got it wrong, either the place or the time, a dark figure stumbled up out of the ditch to her left—a huge, frantic shape emitting guttural noises. She could hear his sounds through the windows, over the din of tree frogs and mosquitoes and cicadas.

Rennie was suddenly there, pulling the extra netting awkwardly over the figure, jerking the car door open, shoving the man in the back seat. The whine of mosquitoes increased as he threw himself into the driver's seat and slammed the car in reverse. He made a less-than-graceful turn in the middle of the narrow dirt track, running backward and forward several times before shifting into low, and roaring back in the direction they had come. The vehicle bounced hard over the ruts, jarring its occupants from side to side.

Another tremendous crack of thunder shook the car and rain came out of nowhere, whiting out the windshield and overwhelming the ineffective wipers.

"We have to get out of here or we're stuck. Even a shower muds this road down in seconds." Rennie shoved his foot harder against the foot feed, and the Packard slid sideways several yards before straightening itself. An animal-like groan came from the back seat.

"Give him the bottle of whiskey," Rennie said to the girl, "and roll down the windows. We'll blow the buggers out before they eat us alive." He flipped the headlights on high.

Wind rushed through the Packard as they neared the asphalt road. The girl's hair flew in all directions, and the rain blew in, soaking her dress. But when the windows were rolled back up a few minutes later, the maddening whine had gone.

This isn't like riding in a car at all, she thought, *it is like being in the stomach of some heaving, putrid beast.*

After another five minutes of furious driving, Rennie braked the car to a fast roll and struggled out of the mosquito netting.

"Can't see a damned thing."

The girl pulled hers off too and darted a glance into the silent back seat. The man, minus netting, was hideous. In the dim light from the dashboard, his face was swollen with pustules and smeared in something thick and black and sickening. The smell oozing out of his clothes and body was that of dead animal.

She watched as he lifted the bottle to where his lips must be and held it there a long time.

"Mosquitoes bore through mud," he said, lowering the bottle and grinning horribly.

"Shouldn't be mosquitoes this time of the year." She said the first thing that came into her head.

"They have no season when it rains inland." The monster's voice was bitter.

The girl shook a Chesterfield out of its tin box and put it in her mouth. She heard the man behind her groan as she dug a matchbook from the bottom of her purse, lit the cigarette, drew in on it and handed it over the back seat.

"Dank . . . thank you."

She lit another one and said, "Rennie?"

Pale-yellow shards of lightening jabbed the sky in front of them and another crash of thunder shook the car.

"Not now," Rennie rubbed a hand across the inside of the

windshield. "I'm driving blind as it is." The wipers swatted back and forth, making little squeaking noises, barely moving the thick, white rain.

She puffed on the cigarette. "Maybe we should pull over. If nobody's looking for him . . ."

"No. We're not to stop until we get home."

"But if we run off the road," she swallowed, "we'll end up looking like him."

"We're not to stop." The inside of the car, already redolent with the odor of sweat, unwashed body and fear, grew increasing musty.

"Damned headlights. If we hadn't had to paint them half black . . ." Rennie giggled suddenly and pushed his foot down on the gas pedal. "Oh, well, maybe we'll outrun it."

The storm stayed with them as they finished the last ten miles to the coast. The man in the back seat was asleep by then, and the girl held her nose and breathed through her mouth.

"You'll never get the car clean," she remarked.

"All part of the adventure, dearie." Rennie giggled again, then sobered. "Watch for other headlights. I'm cutting down Old Dixie Road, and it's officially closed." He switched on the parking lights and shut off the high beams.

"Then why . . .?"

"It'll save five minutes. The new rule says nobody on it from a half hour after sunset to a half hour before sunrise, but they can't patrol it all. They don't have the vehicles." He made the turn and roared down the empty road for several minutes, then skidded off onto another blacktop road and finally onto a two-tracked mud lane.

The rain suddenly lightened, and Rennie let out a long loud breath as they neared the house. He ran the Packard up the driveway, stopped at the garage and got out to open the doors.

When the car was backed safely inside, the three of them—their passenger noticeably limping—hurried across the lawn to the house and in through the unlocked side door.

A voice came out of the darkness. "All right? You found them?"

The monster answered, voice thickening as he explained at length and in German.

"And Wolff was caught," the first voice sounded dispirited as well as disembodied.

The girl snapped on a lamp, and the speaker rose from a chair, eyes flashing blue in the sudden light. He looked at the man, then Rennie and finally at her. "The medicine bag and a very hot bath, yes?"

Rennie gave a shaky laugh. "Just a double bourbon for me, thanks all the same."

Chapter 22

I was up and downstairs the next morning, long before my ten o'clock appointment with Florence DeLong. My face, arms and legs were scratched, and I ached all over, but I was still on an adrenalin high from the night before. Nothing seemed too difficult to tackle. Not even a crotchety old woman who ogled the furniture when she talked to you.

Bear was still sleeping, but Kenji was up and working. He'd promised me prints by late afternoon. I filled a Thermos cup with coffee, shot out the back door and came face to face with Alec Pace. Well, face to face across the empty street.

He was getting out of a jeep in front of his house, a Jeep I'd never seen before, and he was standing there, door still open, looking straight at me.

I wanted to ask him what happened to his pickup and if he'd

been sitting in it on the street two nights earlier, but I didn't. Even from that distance he didn't look good, face too white, eyes tired and circled with gray. Obviously, drinking martinis on his upstairs patio in a divorced state looked a lot better on him than his return to post-marital bliss. But maybe that was just wishful thinking.

"Hey, Alec." I waved a hand and edged sideways in the direction of the garage. Seeing him put serious dents in my euphoria. After all, he'd willingly left me for a proven bitch, which was not a confidence-building thought. "So, how's it going?" I managed a vague, cheerful mutter.

He put on a grin of his own and slammed the Jeep door. "Great. Just stopped by to check out a plumbing problem. You know renters. No mercy." His voice was stranger-pleasant.

"Yeah, right." I waved again, left and got my car. By the time I backed out of the garage, he'd already disappeared. Which was fine with me. I hoped his plumbing problems involved several hundred feet of rusted pipe and he and his ex-wife spent their evenings watching reality TV.

After the Mizner mansion, the townhouses at Little Clam Bay must have seemed like public housing projects to Jerricha's grandmother. They were white, featureless and extremely small. The black baby grand, glued-down keys or not, took up nearly all of the L-shaped dining-living room, but Mrs. DeLong didn't seem to notice. Hot as it was outside, she wore a green coat sweater over a turtleneck and still looked chilled to the bone.

She led me to two easy chairs, in what could have been a den or breakfast room, and poured coffee out of a silver pot into thin china cups without asking if I wanted any. Then she seated herself and waited politely as I opened my notebook and got out a pen.

"I'm glad you didn't bring a tape recorder." Her voice was nearly friendly as she stared out the window. "I don't speak into tape recorders."

"Or talk on video tape?" I figured we may as well get that out of the way.

"Well," she frowned at the arm of her chair. "I never have. They never approved of me, really, so I had to do it all myself."

"Who didn't approve?"

"The historical society people, the ones who try to rewrite history the way they *wish* it had been. They were a very small organization when I came here in the sixties, and they weren't interested in the war. Only in the early settlers, the ones who came in the 1800's and managed to lead lives more boring than Oklahomans. I was an outsider, and they didn't want my help or my viewpoint. So I wrote my own journal."

A smile touched the corner of her mouth. "Money is a bigger asset than talent if you're publishing a history magazine, and I had quite a lot when my husband passed away. I sold the advertising myself and held on until it started paying for itself—about twelve years. After that they changed their minds and actively courted me, but I let them know what I thought of that. Too little too late. Anyway," she looked smug, "I've outlived all of them now."

"The historical society doesn't have anything to do with this project," I assured her. "It's the history *department*—at the college. Grant money."

She sat up straighter in her chair. "That boy was arrogant and stupid. He didn't care about the war; he was only interested in sensation. I refused to talk to him." Her gaze slid to a row of palm trees outside the window. "But I'm happy to help *you* if I can, and perhaps you'll help me too."

I eyed her thoughtfully. Something had shifted her into

good-behavior mode. Maybe her son Tom had put in a word for me. Or maybe she'd just been off her meds last time we met. She was paler than the last time, a little diminished somehow, less energetic.

"I've been reading your articles." I applied butter with a liberal knife. "You really have a gift for creating atmosphere. Tell me about Seminole Beach in the Forties. It was a small town then, only two or three thousand people, correct?"

"Yes, but when I first arrived in the early sixties, the population was larger, around five thousand."

I stopped writing. "Did I misunderstand? I thought you were here in the Forties."

"No, only in Miami with my first husband for a short period of time. They sent him to Officer Candidate School, but he shipped out in nineteen forty-two and was killed. I was expecting Tom by then," her eyes focused on the far wall, "so I went back home to Rhode Island. To my people."

"I see. It's amazing how you got the feel of Seminole Beach in the articles you wrote. I mean, for a northerner who was just in Miami a few months, it was like you lived it. Your description of the heat, the bugs, the blackouts . . ."

"Oh, I was here for that. They didn't enforce the national blackout until late in the war, you know, although some people along the coast had been doing it voluntarily. They had a practice run while I was staying at the Roney Plaza in Miami Beach. Wonderful hotel, the fanciest one in town. Arthur Murray danced there—barefoot on the sand." Her eyes lit up and her face dropped about a dozen years.

"We were out on the terrace—several of my husband's friends and some other people. There were lights in both directions as far as you could see, and then they all went out at the same time, all along the Eastern Seaboard. You were instantly and totally submerged in black. Shocking, in its way, and frightening."

"But you never visited Seminole Beach during the war?"

"No. When I moved here I talked to people who lived through it and wrote several articles about the area. You've probably read the one about the old buildings in town."

I hadn't gotten to that one yet, but I nodded and kept still.

"City Hall, for example, is next to what was then the old Victory Arcade. There was no Riverwalk then, not for another forty years, but if there had been a Riverwalk, the Victory would have sat practically on top of it. The Arcade had a hotel on one side and the first USO canteen on the other. It was very popular with the young servicemen."

I jotted down *Victory Hotel* and *USO*.

"Did you ever know a woman named Eileen Coates? She's about ninety now, I suppose. She told me about the USO dances. Also about people in town smuggling fuel to the German submarines. And spies coming ashore, things like that."

Mrs. DeLong planted a disapproving eye on the palm trees outside her window.

"Nothing like that happened here. The worst people did was drive their cars for pleasure instead of business or ignore the blackout rule, but there's always somebody with a wild story. And some people aren't well mentally. They say anything."

"Okay, tell me how you managed to publish the Sunshine Quarterly single-handedly all those years."

"I did most of the writing myself, until I could get people to contribute articles. And I had a couple of locals to put it together and send it away to be printed. But good help got harder to find; most of them preferred to waitress. Last year it was just me and one girl. That was one of the reasons I decided to stop."

"That was, uh, Cindy Meir? The woman your granddaughter lived with?"

There was a delay before she nodded. "She was with me for over a year. Not a writer or a researcher in any sense of the word, but she understood computers."

"You must have paid her fairly well. Jerricha said she bought a house from you."

Mrs. DeLong's eyes narrowed. "I owned another house, not a particularly good house, but I let her live there as part of her salary. When she evidenced interest in having a place of her own, I gave her excellent terms."

"She must have been a valuable employee."

"Well, she showed up every day, and she wasn't pierced or tattooed anywhere you could see."

I laughed out loud, and she darted a surprised look at the top of my head. Obviously, she hadn't meant to be funny.

"My generation understood hard work and duty." She stood and walked over to a wall of books. "They kept diaries to remind themselves what success involved." She pulled out one of several large, blue-bound volumes. "These are mine. Have you ever seen any of them?"

I was rapidly counting blue books: three full shelves, fifteen per shelf. But her question brought me up short.

How would I have seen them?

"No," I stared at her. "Surely you didn't write all of these during the war?"

She let the book fall open and studied a page. "I started writing in Oklahoma, actually. Tom's stepfather encouraged me to get a degree in literature when our marriage wasn't—a great success. Going to school, keeping a diary; it was good therapy." She paused. "Tom's stepfather didn't want to talk about the war either. He had enough bad memories, he said. Just wanted peace and quiet and meals on time. We could have traveled, but we didn't." Her tone was bitter. "Nothing but remote in Tulsa. Even the air was free."

"I beg your pardon?"

She replaced the blue book and took out another one. "I was always out of breath in the old days. Just from the excitement. White sand beaches, European refugees, nude floor shows, Ciro's, the Casino, fluttering palm trees." Her voice strayed into Elvis-was-an-alien territory, and she swayed slightly from side to side. "In Oklahoma, there was only air. It was free, and there was a lot of it."

"Okay." I looked down at my notebook. "I read in the paper that they found a basement under your house."

That brought her back from wherever she'd gone.

"It was a mistake. I think they meant a sort of buried foundation. I lived in that house forty years. If there had been a basement, I'd have known about it. Anyway, it was covered over this morning." She walked over to the piano, leaned down and stared into the framed photographs on top of it.

I sat still, deciding whether or not to bag it. It was possible that moving out of the house she'd loved for forty years had traumatized her permanently You don't make award-winning videos by exploiting people who are several cheese curls short of a bag. Or at least you shouldn't. Maybe I should forget the two women and finish Joey's nineteen minutes with just Louie Janclowski. I rose slowly and joined her at the piano. There was a new, framed addition since I'd seen her last, a large black-and-white photo taken from the business side of a cocktail bar. Half a dozen servicemen and several women were bellied up on the other side, smiling and smoking cigarettes. One was a twentyish Florence DeLong, hair piled up on her head with white flowers. She was laughing at the only man not in uniform, a dark-haired guy in a light-colored suit. A slash of thick, flowing script across the right-hand corner read: Fun, Fun, Yours, Rennie.

"I like your pictures," I pointed at the man in the suit. "Your first husband?"

"Oh, no, just a very dear friend."

I glanced around the room. "Did you hang your painting? The one of you in a red dress? With the pirates on the wall?"

"I have nothing like that." Her eyes were still on the photograph. "I like to have all my pictures around me. When you get to a certain age, the dead are much more real than the living."

Okay, then. I tucked my notebook back in my purse. I was definitely bagging it. "Well, thanks for talking to me. It was very helpful. Maybe—"

"I keep everything I ever wrote too." She turned and looked me straight in the eye. "What do you think of people who read a person's private thoughts? Shouldn't they be returned to the rightful owner? Just as a matter of decency?"

The sound of a door opening interrupted her, and a man's voice called, "Where are you?"

Florence DeLong looked up expectantly as her son entered the room. Tom Roddler's eyes flicked from the blue book she was holding, to me, then back again.

"Do you think this is wise?" he said calmly.

She put the book back on the shelf and drew her shoulders up. "Well, it was your idea. You said I should have talked to the girl, that she was harmless."

"I'm sorry," Tom Roddler held the edge of my car door and stood looking down at me. "It's just—she doesn't always know what she's saying. She gets the past confused with what she's read. You can't be sure she's telling you things that actually happened."

I stared straight out the windshield, face still burning. "Listen, I don't have to be escorted out of any place. Your mother called *me*. She *wanted* to be interviewed. I thought she'd be a—a wealth of information. It didn't occur to me you'd object."

"It isn't like that. I don't. I don't object, exactly."

"What, then?"

"I told you, my mother seems okay, but she isn't always. Was she reading them to you? The blue books?"

I shook my head.

"She didn't talk about my father?"

"She talked about your stepfather. She said the marriage didn't work out."

His hand dropped away from the car door. "Work out? It certainly did not. She hated Oklahoma and everything in it, him included, and she didn't hesitate to tell him every chance she got." He took in a breath and let it out slowly. "Did she tell you he drank himself to death? Did she tell you she was in and out of mental hospitals for years, on and off medication, addicted to this thing and that, ballet dancing for twelve hours at a time, painting for days with no sleep? And that after he died and we moved here, she narrowed it down to only one addiction: writing those stupid stories for that fucking magazine? Did she tell you she did it day and night for forty years like it was the only thing that mattered? That nothing mattered except her stupid stories?"

My own anger was pretty much eaten up by his. "No, she didn't say any of those things."

He opened his mouth and closed it again. A bleak smile turned up the edge of his mouth, and for a second he looked like his mother. "No, of course not. Sorry again. It's been a rough week."

"Look," I reached out a hand, then thought better of it, "I don't know what you . . . I mean, your family life, good or bad, doesn't come into it. I couldn't use much of what she told me today anyway. The video is just interviews with people who remember the war and want to talk about it." A voice in my head was chanting, *Liar, liar, pants on fire*, as I remembered last night's trip to the basement and Eileen Coates. I ignored it and took refuge in near-truth. "Your mother wasn't even in Seminole Beach during the Forties."

He looked down at the ground. "What was she saying about the diaries?"

I shrugged. "Something about people who read your personal thoughts. She was a little odd about it."

After a moment he looked up and smiled at me. His eyes looked tired.

"This wasn't the conversation I intended to have next time I saw you." He reached out and pushed a strand of hair behind my ear. "I was thinking more like drinks, dinner, maybe a wild night on the town. You think you could do that next week? When I get my schedule pinned down?"

"Maybe." I leaned my head back against the seat, away from him. "I have to tell you, though, I'm not real good with drama anymore. It wears me out."

He cupped the palm of his hand around the side of my neck and kept it there for a minute. "Okay. Just don't count me out. Okay?"

I watched as he walked to his car and got in behind the wheel. This time he hadn't dropped his aide downtown. Old Sherry was sitting tall in the passenger seat of the black Lexus, glaring at me.

Chapter 23

Kenji had photographs spread all over the kitchen worktable when I got back to the house. Some were useless, merely white-bordered rectangles of mottled gray and black, but there were half a dozen reasonably good prints—a miracle, really, since he'd shot them twenty feet away, at an angle, hanging upside down in a hole.

I studied an eight-by-ten color shot that clearly showed pirates. They were caricatures, cartoonish, larger-than-life men burying treasure, hauling wooden kegs, sword fighting. Two of them swung from ropes with women, in fancy dresses, draped over their arms. One had a knife between his teeth.

"Amazing." I said to Kenji. "How'd you manage to get around the mildew and peeling paint?"

He looked smug and didn't answer.

I looked closely at the rope-swinging pirates. The one chewing a knife had pale-yellow hair and bright-blue eyes. The woman draped over his arm was dark haired with a lot of cleavage and a long, red dress. The second woman, a blondish-brunette, was being abducted by a guy wearing an eye patch and a knotted head scarf. She didn't look like she was offended. A huge gold chain with a letter L dangled from her neck

"I can't believe the colors," I said to Kenji. "Did you enhance them?"

He shook his head. "New paint, maybe."

"What? Somebody painted these recently?"

"Or re-painted."

A long section of bar was visible in two of the photos. It looked like the one in Florence DeLong's oil painting. The one of her in the red dress that she claimed not to have.

I switched my attention to the pictures of U-boats. There were two sets, but the colored prints were useless. Even the black and whites were faded and partially obliterated.

"Water damage," Kenji remarked, watching me. "Not re-painted. Got only five shots before *real* shooting starts." He grinned at his own joke.

Someone had painted a thick, meandering outline of the Florida peninsula and placed U-boats along both east and west coasts. The subs had names and numbers, mostly unreadable. The clearest looked like U-5-6, -/3/42, Oce-n Venu-.

"Ocean Venus? Seems a little feminine for a U-boat," I said to Kenji.

He shook his head and handed me a computer printout. "I looked up boats sunk off Florida by German wolf pack. One is Ocean Venus, May 3, 1942 by U-boat 546."

I slid my finger quickly down Kenji's list. Over two dozen freighters and tankers from Sweden, Britain, Panama, the

Netherlands, and the U.S. had been torpedoed between February of 1942 and April of 1943. U-boat 123 was the undisputed winner. It had knocked off four freighters all by itself in as many days.

I frowned at Kenji. "Ben said this kind of information was kept out of the papers. Who painted the U-boats on the wall then?"

"I don't know. Someone who keeps track?"

No towns or roads had been marked on the Florida map, but giant letters had been printed across its center: N-E-U-E-S-D-E-U-T-SC-H-L-A-N-D. I waved the print at him

"Doesn't that mean New Germany?"

Kenji nodded. "Study German in school."

I took two of the pirate prints and one of the U-boat prints and slid them into a large envelope.

"Hang on to the rest, okay? I have to run an errand."

Once again I didn't bother calling the care facility. I was too busy thinking up questions I wanted to ask Eileen Coates. Like, did she hang out at Florence DeLong's Mizner house back in the Forties? Like, was she the woman on the pirate wall with the initial-L necklace, and, if so, who painted those pictures? She said a man had called her Lena. I hoped she'd be clear-headed enough to answer. And to sweeten the pot, I was returning her swastika. I flew out to Park Place in less than ten minutes, presented myself at the desk and asked to see Mrs. Coates.

The same pleasant, thirtyish woman I'd met before smiled at me and shook her head. "I'm afraid you can't—"

"It's important," I said. "She gave me something to hold for her. I want to return it."

"I'll be happy to take it for you," the woman said, "but I'm afraid it's not possible—"

"Look, it's very important," I fingered the envelope of photographs. "If she's busy or something, I'll wait, but I have to see her."

The woman shook her head again. "What I'm trying to say is that it's not possible to see Mrs. Coates at all. I'm afraid she passed away in the night."

"Passed away?"

"Well, dear, she was very old. It wasn't unexpected, you know."

I didn't give her the iron cross. I don't entrust personal belongings to thirty-year-olds who call me dear. I drove out of the parking lot in such a daze that a pick-up truck nearly clipped me. Even that didn't clear my head or help me figure out what to do next. I couldn't think of anything except a question I should have asked the receptionist: Had Eileen Coates had a visitor the day she died? One with a web tattoo on his hand?

On the way home I tried to still the wild ideas popping around in my head. Was something really going on or had I just watched too many *Matlock* reruns? Why had Ben's friend, Joey, chucked the project and left the country if he thought he'd unearthed a scandal? Did he discover there wasn't one?

There isn't any scandal, Keegan, just a bunch of silliness. Aunt Bridgie's voice sliced through my self-talk. *So what if somebody stole a nineteen forty-three newspaper's microfilm from the library? Happens every day—just like some lay-about swiped the recorder out of your car as he wandered by.*

But what about the iron cross?

What of it? You can buy one in any flea market.

Well, somebody painted those U-boats in Florence DeLong's basement forty years ago.

Ridiculous. Everybody in Seminole Beach knew about the German submarines. Somebody did it for fun. God knows there wasn't much entertainment around here in the Forties. If it was even painted in the Forties.

"But Eileen Coates died last night. Suddenly!" I protested aloud.

I could feel her sigh of disgust. *She was ninety-three years old, for heaven's sake. She was lucky to live that long.*

"Florence DeLong lied about the pirate pictures," I said stubbornly. "Somebody painted her in front of that wall sixty years ago, and she lied about it."

Ladies are not required to answer questions truthfully when it's no one's business.

I turned left on East River Road. "Okay, okay, maybe. But somebody did shoot at Kenji and me while he was taking pictures of the basement."

You were trespassing on a work site, Keegan. That's against the law. That's why they hire guards: to keep people from stealing equipment.

"So," I said, still out loud, now frustrated, "none of it means anything, and there's no point in going to the police?"

Good Lord, no. What would the neighbors think? I'm sure any photojournalist, pardon me, former photojournalist, worth her salt knows how to make something out of nothing. However, you live in this town, and I cannot imagine upsetting the descendants of anyone involved just to enhance a second-rate video that's of limited interest to anyone.

I was in a very bad mood as I put the car in the garage. It's not every day you get argued to the mat by a dead person. However, as soon as I entered the kitchen, I discovered a brand-new crisis. Jerricha had left the house around ten that morning without a word to anyone and hadn't returned.

Two calls had come for her in the afternoon, both demanding that she come to the phone. The voice was the same: loud, female and angry to the point of ranting.

Nita, who took the calls, was upset because Jerricha had disappeared and might be in trouble; Jesse was upset because she disappeared without saying where she was going; Bear and Kenji were upset because she disappeared without making dinner.

I didn't consider missing a meal a crisis, let alone my problem, but it was clear that Bear and Kenji did. They sat at the kitchen table drinking coffee long after Nita and Jesse left, and discussed it in depressed voices. I listened for about ten minutes before deciding not to return to the days of post-Amy anarchy. Also, I owed both of them for our late-night boat trip. I checked the refrigerator, found a large package of chicken breasts thawing on a platter and went to Amy's bookshelves to look for a recipe.

Dinner in Half an Hour or Less looked like the answer. As I pulled it off the shelf the jacket came off in my hand, and the book inside fell to the floor.

The book seemed a lot older than its jacket. It had a red, water-stained cover and no title on the spine. The pages were yellow, handwritten in pencil and coming loose from the binding. Old recipes from Amy's family who'd once owned a restaurant? I read the first page and saw it wasn't.

"It's a B-29. Try it, you'll love it . . ."

I flipped through the pages, my eyes skimming down the lines: "That's why I like having you around, darling. You reject bullshit out of hand and you introduce me to so many handsome men. . . . My God Florence, can't you entertain yourself for one evening? Don't argue. . . . You're a fool, Florence. We'll have to siphon extra gas out of the Packard."

They seemed to be journal entries, all of them, written in the early months of 1943. Some of the phrasing was very familiar, and I was pretty sure where I'd seen it before.

"Back in a minute, Bear." I left the chicken on the counter and ran up the mezzanine stairs. The articles I'd copied from Florence DeLong's *Sunshine Quarterly* were still in a pile on the bed. I spread them out and started matching diary entries to magazine articles. The one about the national blackout began, word for word, exactly like the journal entry.

In another entry, dated March 6, 1943, a man named Rennie and a female companion rescued an escaping POW from a drainage ditch several miles inland. The POW's face was covered in mud and insect bites. A corresponding magazine article explained how prisoners in a nearby POW camp were transported to orange groves within a dozen miles of Seminole Beach to pick fruit. The descriptions were the same: rutted mud roads, humpbacked bridges and mosquitoes.

I closed the red book carefully. It had apparently provided the raw material for the articles Florence DeLong wrote about World War II. Or was it the other way around?

I slid the pile of photocopies and the journal under my mattress and hustled back downstairs. For some reason, Jerricha had swiped and hidden her grandmother's diary. That was why Florence De Long asked if I'd seen it. But the books Mrs. DeLong had shown me were blue—and this one was red. Even stranger, all the entries in the red book were written in the third person.

Like a novel.

Chapter 24

I never did find *Meals in Thirty Minutes or Less*, and Jerricha didn't show up for dinner, but we managed to eat on schedule. I followed an old recipe of Amy's that called for ingredients we had on hand: ginger, orange juice, red wine and honey, instant rice and some frozen baby peas. I tossed crackers and cheese on the worktable for Bear and Kenji, who shifted from coffee to beer. I also chilled a couple of bottles of white burgundy in case the chicken had been out on the counter too long. Nothing like alcohol to counteract the effects of acute salmonella.

The tenants ate everything without comment, except for Jesse, but his complaints weren't food related. He was worried, out-loud worried, about Jerricha and where and why she had gone.

I was anxious to get back upstairs to the rest of Florence DeLong's journal, so I more or less ignored Jesse. Jerricha was twenty-four years old, for heaven's sake. She'd turn up when she turned up.

When Nita and Kenji offered to clean the kitchen afterward, I left them to it and shot up to the mezzanine.

It didn't take long to finish reading the faded, red book. And afterward I understood why Mrs. DeLong feared it falling into the wrong hands. I also understood why her son Tom didn't want her talking to me. Assuming it was all true, of course, and Mrs. DeLong wasn't just another old woman who might or might not have slipped a cog.

I couldn't use any part of her journal for Ben's project—well, not and sleep nights. The only solution was to stick it in a padded envelope and mail it back anonymously. Still, I wanted to talk to somebody about it. Somebody who wasn't involved and didn't give a damn. For one brief, insane moment, I nearly looked up Alec's ex-wife's phone number and called him. He was on the outside; he could certainly tell me what not to do. I paced from room to room, thinking up ideas and rejecting them, then realized my pacing range was way too limited. I needed wide-open spaces.

I shoved my driver's license and a couple of dollars in the pocket of my shorts, grabbed my car keys and headed to the beach. That was better than the Riverwalk; no dead bodies there, just the comforting sound of waves and a breeze at least five degrees cooler than the one in town. However, as I crossed the causeway bridge, I got an even brighter idea. The ocean could be lonely and creepy at night, and the sun would soon be going down. The fancy new causeway bridge had lights and a wide, pedestrian walkway. Even better, the herds of people who went huffing and puffing up and down its sixty-five foot span dwindled to a trickle after seven o'clock. I'd feel safe and still be alone enough to think.

I drove into a nearby parking lot, sprayed my arms and legs with mosquito repellent from the glove compartment, and started up the ramp.

I was one of many people who voted against building the new bridge. My theory was simple: As soon as you started repairing the roads and doing away with drawbridges, a whole lot of tourists moved to town who'd be just as happy somewhere else. However, the finished product was beautiful—for a bridge— and the view from the top was spectacular as long as you didn't look straight down. I've never been good with heights.

I swung my arms and thought about Florence DeLong.

She had lied about the basement. Lied about the portrait of her painted in front of the pirate wall. Lied about knowing Eileen Coates. Maybe she lied in the diary too; simply made it up out of all that free, Oklahoma air. After all, she'd spent a lot of time in mental hospitals, according to her son. But what if the journal entries were true? Should she be punished? And for what? Consorting with the enemy over half a century ago? Politics were different in the new millennium. In spite of Tom Roddler's opinion, Arnold Schwarzenegger had done all right in California, and nobody cared who his father was. Hell, even a recent pope had been a member of Hitler Youth. Would anybody really be bothered over a sixty-year-old love affair?

I stopped to rest, leaned against the chest-high railing and stared out at the river. Two motorboats raced out from under the bridge, trailing white foam wakes, and the sun laid coppery-gold streaks across the water. The air wasn't as humid this high up, and with every breath my head got clearer. It wasn't 1943 anymore, and Florence DeLong wasn't a restless young woman. She was a very old lady with a solid reputation as a historian. She obviously hadn't stolen my notes or the microfilm or fired a shotgun at me. I breathed in some more. Walking the bridge had been a good choice. Not even one car had passed me on the way up.

On the heels of that thought, a green Ford came flying up behind me and stopped on the other side of the cement divider. The guy in the passenger seat threw open the door, jumped out and vaulted over the low cement wall. At the same time, the driver ran around behind the car and jumped the wall to my left. In the seconds it took to realize I was boxed in—the idling car in front of me, the river behind me and each of them blocking the walkway—I recognized them. The driver was the one with the tattoo on his thumb: Web Boy. The other one, with sleepy eyes, had turned Kenji and me away from the Mizner basement and probably shot at us later the same night.

"What do you want?" My voice cracked as I ground the words out. Fear will do that. I darted a look in one direction, then the other. Where was a car, bicycle, pedestrian, school bus, skateboarder when you really needed one?

"What do we want?" Web Boy grinned at me. "We want you to take a swim." He glanced at the other man. "Count of three, over the side. Ready?"

Sleepy Eyes looked startled. "I thought—don't we just tell her. . . .?"

Web Boy's smile got nastier. "If we just tell you nice to stop making your fucking documentary, will you quit? Or do we throw your ass off the fucking bridge?"

I backed up, or tried to back up. The railing pressed hard into my shoulder blade.

"Are you crazy? What's it to you anyway?"

"I told you." He shook his head at sleepy eyes. "You just can't give some people a break." He turned and screamed in my face. "I followed your car, bitch, and I flushed your tape recorder. Stop making the fucking documentary. Mind your own fucking business! Send that fucking girl back where she belongs! We know she's got the book. Tell her to give it back!"

I shrunk back, away from the combined assault of noise and booze-breath, and his smile got wider.

"We hung your buddy Joey out his condo window and trashed his precious research. He got smart and left town, but you're not that smart, are you? Ready?" He brushed his palms together and made a hideous face at me. "Over you go!"

As Sleepy Eyes took a step forward, I moved. I grabbed the pole with the no-parking sign, jumped to the top of the divider and threw myself across the top of their car. My leg scraped the cement wall and pain fired through my ankle. Somebody grabbed my shoe, but I was going so fast it came off as I slid over the car roof and half jumped, half fell onto the roadway.

I dashed across the two westbound lanes, praying for a vehicle of any kind. Somebody yelled "Fucker!" way too close to the back of my head, and I ran harder, scraping both hands on the second divider as I vaulted into the eastbound lanes. I veered right and headed straight up the white line, wondering how far I'd get before they caught me. If I stayed in the middle, they might pound me, but that was better than being thrown down, down, down to the water. The thought of falling sixty screaming feet was more than I could handle. I could hear them getting closer, swearing and breathing hard, and my one bare foot was being banged to death on the pavement. I kicked in the last bit of energy I had and swerved like a manic linebacker, back toward the wall that divided the four lanes.

A second later the roof of a pickup truck popped over the crest of the bridge nearly in my face. It was doing at least fifty when it blew by with a foot to spare. Then there was a thump

166   False Impression

and the sound of screeching brakes as the truck skidded down the pavement and smashed to a stop against the divider. By the time the driver opened his door and all but fell out, the green Ford was flying in the opposite direction and Sleepy Eyes was gone, leaving his buddy, web tattoo and all, face down on the cement.

As a famous man once remarked, it was déjà vu all over again. Detective DeCicero and I faced each other across his plastic wood-grain desk, he asked questions, and I answered. Only this time I took the coffee he offered. I needed it.

"They just told you to quit making a documentary, that was it?"

I nodded and swallowed hot tasteless black liquid. "They were going to throw me off the bridge. The guy before me got dangled out his apartment window."

"Over a video tape about World War II?"

"I guess. They also said they destroyed his research, but I've got a box of stuff they missed. He left that at the college."

"I'd like to look at it. When we finish here, I'll drive by your house and pick it up."

"Sure." I tried to set the paper cup down on the desk, but my hand wobbled and I changed my mind. "I think the tattooed kid was on something—drugs, maybe just booze. He smelled like it. The other one kind of did what the tattooed one said."

DeCicero eyed me thoughtfully. "There must be something you're not telling me. Too much of a coincidence that a guy hanging around the park when you discover a body tries to throw you off a bridge a couple weeks later "

My mouth opened in surprise. "I forgot about Robbie Garcia."

"You know his name?"

"I read it in the paper."

"Mmmh. And you're sure you didn't see anything that day? Didn't forget to mention something that happened?"

"There wasn't anything. Honestly." I hesitated for a second, wondering what he'd say if I told him about Bear and the Trimaran, but that was only one of Bear's theories. Besides, why rat out Bear when I wasn't going to admit trespassing at Florence DeLong's basement myself?

DeCicero frowned at me. "Sometimes people forget. For instance, you didn't tell me about Jerricha Roddler."

"What about her?"

"She's living in your house."

"Yes, but . . ." I stopped. "How'd you know that?"

"She got picked up for DUI, and the guy she called—the guy who came to bail her out—is one of your tenants."

"Who?"

He looked down at a note pad by his elbow. "Jesse Schraft. You told me you didn't know Jerricha."

"I didn't. We ran into each other downtown at the coffee shop *after* I talked to you. She said she wouldn't go back where she was living. I felt sorry for her and said she could stay at the house in exchange for some work. She cooks."

"Cooks." He looked at me like I was an idiot.

I set the paper cup down with both hands and slid back in the chair. "Our other cook is away for a few weeks. Jerricha's filling in."

"Okay. Let's get back to the bridge."

He ran through the questions again. Why was I walking there at that time of night? What did each of the men who accosted me say? Why did I think they cared about a video tape?

I didn't tell him what they said about Jerricha; in fact, I left her out completely. Partly because she was in enough trouble, partly because I didn't think it was fair to Tom Roddler, and partly because of her grandmother's little red book. I wasn't a big Florence DeLong fan, but I agreed with her on one point: Her journal was nobody else's business.

DeCicero looked at his watch. "Okay, Mrs. Shaw. I'll be talking to you again. You call me if you think of anything you haven't mentioned." He handed me another one of his cards. "You sure you're okay?"

I glanced at my scraped hands. "Yeah. It doesn't seem real. What are you going to do?"

His eyebrows lifted. "Excuse me?"

"I mean, the people at the college aren't going to be happy if there's a lot of negative publicity about their project. And I might like to keep my job, part time or not. I'm hoping my name's not going to be in the paper."

"Right now it's down as an accident under investigation. We won't release any information until we find out what's going on."

"And you think there's a connection between Robbie Garcia and these two guys?"

He shrugged. "Don't know. I'd ask your tattooed friend if it was possible."

"He's not dead is he?"

He shook his head. "But he's gonna be a long time getting back to normal."

Chapter 25

DeCicero offered to take me back to my car after he picked up Ben's box of materials, but the BMW was safe where it was for a while, and I had something to take care of at home.

I went up to the mezzanine without encountering anyone, took a very hot shower and waited for post-bridge-attack stress to kick in. When it didn't I decided all that running must have burned up my store of flight-or-fight energy. Several new aches and pains had been added to the ones acquired at Mrs. De-Long's basement, but I couldn't feel any fear anywhere. Why wasn't I shaking like a leaf or throwing up from sheer relief?

Because Web Boy is out of circulation, the voice in my head sounded like my ex. *He went from being ominously everywhere—following you on a bike, visiting Eileen Coates, shooting at you, threatening bodily harm—to a harmless,*

169

greasy spot on the bridge. He's the only one who really scared you; Sleepy Eyes and Cindy Meir are all puff and no substance in your mind. You never learn, Keegan, you have no brain.

I started humming loudly to tune him out. It sounded like the theme from Indiana Jones. Maybe I should see somebody about the voices.

I sprayed Bactine on the new scratches on my arms and legs, put on clean clothes, fished the red journal out from under my mattress and went downstairs. In the refrigerator I found an open bottle of merlot and chugged down a cupful. Then I headed to the sun porch.

Jerricha was there, as I expected, lying on Jesse's austere version of a bed, a tall, narrow, wood box attached to one wall with a thin mattress on top. In spite of the heat and Jesse's lack of air conditioning, she had a thermal blanket pulled all the way up to her chin. Her eyes were yellowish, only half open, and she looked like she had the flu.

"I heard you bailed her out," I said to Jesse, who stood beside the bed watching her. "Why'd she call you?"

"Why not?" He was staring down at her like he was—a word flitted through my head—besotted. A second later I realized I was correct; Bear hadn't been the one to worry about, it was Jesse.

"What'd she do it on? Booze or drugs?"

Jesse kept staring. "Does it matter? This is just how she's learned to process the missteps in her life . . ."

"Right." I interrupted before I got the full lecture. I leaned over Jerricha and held up the red book. "It was a good idea, unless somebody wanted to cook something in a hurry."

She didn't say anything, but her eyes got wider.

"You put it there the morning you were 'sorting Amy's

books by color.' Why? Why steal your grandmother's journal?"

Jerricha twisted her head a little. "Is that what it is?"

"Obviously. Since her name is in it and dates and—"

Her lip threatened to pout itself right off her face. "I told you. I don't read real good, and it was cursive. It looked like a story. And it was so old."

"That wasn't the question. Why'd you take it?"

"I didn't!" Her eyes were angry but her voice dropped to a whisper. "Cindy did."

"Cindy Meir? C'mon, Jerricha, I've been hearing Cindy stories since you moved in here. Why would she want it?"

"I don't know," she said defiantly. "I don't! I just know that after she got it, Grandmother let her stay in the house for free. And let her buy it real cheap."

"And paid your rent to her anyway?"

She nodded, her eyes on the book. "I took it to give it back. To Grandmother, but I haven't seen her."

"Sure you have."

"I forgot it the day we went over there."

"So the threatening calls were from Cindy? Wanting it back?"

She hesitated and then nodded.

"And if you don't hand it over, then what?"

"She'll ruin my whole family."

"So you flipped out and got wasted?"

Jesse picked up a nasty-looking cup of his personally concocted brown liquid and held it to her lips. "She really should rest. She's going to feel worse tomorrow."

"Yeah." I watched her sip at the brown stuff. "You know a kid with a web tattoo on his right hand?"

"No!" She sputtered into the cup. "Well, yeah. Chaz. Cindy's boyfriend."

"You knew that was him? In the park that day? So, did you know the dead guy too and just forget to mention it?"

"She wouldn't know." Jesse set the cup on the floor. "She never saw him."

I shifted my eyes to him. "Okay, I forgot she stayed up in the park." I went back to her. "He was thin, with long, blondish hair, a scraggly sort of beard. Does that sound like one of Cindy's boyfriends?"

Jerricha blinked her eyes. "Like her brother."

"Robbie Garcia was Cindy's brother?" As soon as I said it, Cindy's last name clicked with me. Meir. The same as Robbie's half brother. Bear had told me about talking to him, but I'd missed the connection.

"But you—why didn't you tell somebody about this guy, Chaz?"

"I just forgot about it, okay? He rode up on his bike when I was running. You know, looking for a phone. And I'm like, 'Somebody got hurt,' and he's like, 'Forget it, calm down.' And he, uh, he gave me some stuff and told me to keep my mouth shut."

"What kind of stuff?"

"Pills," she mumbled it into the blanket. "So I went in the coffee place, you know, Spike O's, and waited 'til he went away. He always gives me the creeps." She looked out of the corner of her eyes at Jesse. "And then I remembered I was supposed to find a phone, but I didn't have any money, so I thought I better come back to the park and tell you, so I did."

Jesse frowned at me, but I wasn't through.

"You took his pills, though, right? That's why you were so calm at the coffee shop later. Okay, tomorrow, when you're feeling better, we'll go see Cindy."

"What?" Her eyes were huge.

"You and I will go talk to Cindy."

"But . . . what for?"

"To get her recipe for fried chicken." I said impatiently. "C'mon, Jerricha, use your head. She's right in the middle of everything. It's pretty clear why she wants the journal back, but I want to know what her brother Robbie was doing down on the dock with a bunch of cocaine cookies and why her friend Chaz wanted me to do a swan dive into the river."

Jerricha seemed to sink farther down into the covers. "I'm not messing with Chaz. He's crazy."

"Well, I guess you're in luck then. Old Chaz got hit by a truck tonight. He won't be out of the hospital for a long time."

Jerricha blinked and sucked in a breath, Then, "Nothing to do with me. I won't be around much longer anyway. I'm going in the army."

"The army!" Clearly, Jesse hadn't heard this plan before. "What if you get sent to Afghanistan? You could get killed."

"Not *that* army," she said scornfully, "I'm not going to any war, I'm going in the *other* army, the one with the free education."

Jesse's eye caught mine, and silence stretched out between us.

"Anyway," Jerricha's bottom lip pushed out, "I don't know where Cindy is."

I grinned at her. "Then we'll have to do our best to figure it out. I'll bet you can think of some places to look if you really try, and I'll just sit here until you do." I dropped onto a wooden chair and switched my grin to Jesse. "You got anything to read? I've got nowhere to go and all day to think about it."

It took twenty minutes, but eventually she got tired of looking at me.

"Boobie's," she muttered finally, "she likes Boobie's."

Chapter 26

The Booby Trap was a dump. It was a long, one-story, wooden building off State Road 43 in the middle of orange groves still owned by relatives of the old Alton family. In its last incarnation, it was the Cracker Cafe, specializing in wild hog, swamp cabbage and key lime pie. The current owners had forgone structural or cosmetic renovation and blown the budget on a computerized sign that flashed in purple neon:

Welcome to Boobies!
See Muffie, Kittie, Brandie and Woofie

You could have bought the building and the land it stood on for maybe fifty bucks. The sign would have set you back several thousand.

I parked in the lot beside a sagging, dented bus. Its flamingo-pink paint nearly covered the name of the previous owner—the local school district. "Ladies Ride Free" was spray-painted along the side in tasteful maroon.

I glanced over at Jerricha. "You're absolutely sure Cindy comes to this place?"

"Yeah." She still looked pale and kind of pasty from her DUI experience. "We shouldn't be here. The girls who work here are bad. One of the dancers has 'Your Mama' tattooed inside her bottom lip."

"Well, its male-stripper night, so she won't be dancing, right?"

She looked away. She was pissed because I'd pried the name of Cindy's favorite hangout out of her when she was too sick to resist—even more pissed that I insisted she come along and point Cindy out.

"We shoulda brought Jesse," she pouted. "Even if Chaz isn't around, she's got other guys she can get to help her."

"Look, it won't take ten minutes. If Cindy's here, I'll ask her a few questions, and we'll leave. She can't do anything in a place this crowded, and we'll be halfway home before she whips out her cell phone and calls for reinforcements."

Jerricha merely glowered.

The Booby Trap was dark inside and it smelled damp. We stepped into a long, low room with rows of folding metal chairs and a makeshift stage. The chairs were filled with women drinking plastic cups of beer. They were singing "All My Ex's Live in Texas" along with the jukebox. Thick fog rose up about three feet off the packed-dirt floor, smoking lazily around the chairs and obliterating the women's legs. The room looked like one of the rings of hell.

"How do they do that?" I put a tentative foot into the fog and watched my sandal disappear.

"Dry ice," Jerricha pushed hair back behind one ear and

sounded almost animated. "It's cheaper than those machines. They put it on the floor and spray water on it. Kind of sexy, huh?"

"Gives me the creeps. You see Cindy anywhere?"

"She's always on the front row," Jerricha's eyes raked the crowd. "She broke a blood vessel in her palm once after clapping for some guys dressed up like cable repairmen. Couldn't use that hand for weeks."

"I'll remember to curb my enthusiasm."

A few seconds later the canned music halted, a stocky guy in a T-shirt and khaki shorts jumped up on the stage, and the crowd obediently hushed. I led the way to two empty seats in the back row and sat down gingerly, inches above the dingy white fog. I hoped they had a good exterminator.

"Ladies—and ladies!" The stocky guy cackled at his own wit. "Tonight we bring you—straight from Chicago, Illinois— the most incredible act ever! Put your hands together for Jason and his buddy, Bo-Bo!" He flipped his fingers out several times, and the familiar fog materialized on the stage floor. It steamed up about a foot high and stayed there.

There was a clatter of applause, some loud whistles and a few shouts of "Yo baby!" as a cowboy bounded up onto the stage. He wore tight Levis tucked into tooled-leather boots, a long-sleeved shirt with pearl buttons and a ten-gallon hat. Around his neck hung two ends of the world's biggest python.

There was a loud collective hiss from the audience when they realized the snake was real, and somebody up front let out a shriek. Jason grinned and shouted over the bedlam: "Ladies, my little friend Bo-Bo wouldn't hurt a fly!" He picked up the snake with both hands and lifted it high above his head. "Not only that, he was just fed!"

There was nervous laughter and a few "Bring it ons!" as he lowered the snake to his shoulders and stripper music, heavy on the bass, blasted out over the room. He gyrated back and forth in time to the beat, twirling the snake's tail 'round and 'round.

Jerricha tapped my arm. "There's Cindy."

"Where?" I kept one eye on Bo-Bo and half turned.

"Second row. See? Reddish-blonde hair, kind of curly and sticking out?"

"The one in the black tank top? That's the evil Cindy? She looks harmless from here. Better wait 'til he takes a break. We don't want to start a riot."

At that moment, Jason jerked his hat off a totally bald head and snap-wristed it into the crowd. A heavy woman, who looked about sixty, wrestled it away from a teenager, clapped it on her own head and held onto it with both hands.

Another roar went up as Jason unbuttoned his shirt and did a hip-thrust at the woman wearing his hat. Then the shirt followed the hat into the crowd, and he began undoing his belt buckle. The noise was deafening as he unsnapped his jeans and edged the zipper down.

"Take 'em off! Clear off!" screamed the woman in front of me, waving two twenty dollar bills. "Gimme them pants!"

The jeans slid down his thighs, past his knees and stopped at the top of his boots. For a second, I watched, mesmerized. The boy had something beside himself stuffed into those tiny, red, European undies. Then my gaze shifted lower. His jeans were tight and narrow legged—no way they were coming off over his boots.

Jason's eyes blinked rapidly as he realized his mistake. *Boots off first, boots off first*, he seemed to be thinking. He twirled the boa's tail again, reached down and snatched off a boot. It went arcing through the air into the arms of the woman sitting next to Cindy. She writhed with ecstasy, but I thought it was premature. Better wait 'til she had the pair.

The second boot was harder. Jason stumbled, grabbed at it twice and fell to one knee. The crowd screamed louder, assuming it was part of the act.

And then as Jason stood up, someone noticed Bo-Bo was no longer draped around his shoulders.

Real screams replaced lustful ones as eighty women, sitting up to their waist in impenetrable fog, realized the boa constrictor had disappeared. Metal chairs flew backward as they ran shrieking and shoving for the door.

I wasn't too worried because I figured Bobo would devour the front two rows first, but Cindy had disappeared in the crowd. I pointed to the red exit sign on the far wall and yelled "Let's go out that way if the door's not locked!"

"It's not!" Jerricha shouted back. "Cindy went out it a minute ago!"

"What? Why didn't you say so? Come on!"

The two of us ran to the right as everybody else in the room piled through the door on the left. I stepped out the exit door, down to a cement block and down again to a sandy, junk-filled yard.

"That's her!" Jerricha shouted, close behind me. "Getting in the car."

I pounded through the parking lot and caught up with Cindy just as she threw her size-fourteen butt—crammed into size-ten shorts—into a green Ford. I grabbed the car door before she could pull it shut.

She glared at me, then did a double-take and glared some more. "What the hell do you want? You caused enough trouble sticking your nose in."

"I want to know why you sent your friend Chaz to throw me off a bridge." My voice sounded meaner than I had hoped. "And why Florence DeLong pays you ridiculous rent for Jerricha to live in her own house."

"Hey, she said I could have it. And when I needed some cash, she sent her idiot granddaughter to live there. She wanted it that way."

"Because you had the red book and were blackmailing her? Or was it something else?"

Cindy's face screwed into a smirk. "You been watchin' too much TV. If you're smart, you'll throw the chick out. She's nothing but trouble, and a liar besides. Her whole family's crazy, especially the old witch. Writing those blue books is all that keeps her alive. That and the booze. Same stories over and over, but sometimes the guy leaves her, sometimes he stays. Sometimes he just disappears. Even she don't know what really happened."

I didn't try to keep the scorn out of my voice. "But I'll bet you read every version, right? And then you took the red one—the original—the one that really counted."

She jerked the door out of my hand and slammed it shut "You tell Jerricha," she waved a hand over my right shoulder, "she's got until tomorrow to give me back my property or I tell the cops she killed my fucking brother!" She revved the engine and screeched out of the parking lot.

I turned to say something to Jerricha, but she wasn't there. Old Jerricha had disappeared faster than Bo-Bo the snake.

"You were a lot of help," I complained as we drove home. "What if I'd needed back-up?"

"I went to look for somebody." Jerricha wiggled in her seat. "In case she really went crazy. Cindy's not afraid of me."

"A little late," I said. "What if she was armed or something?"

"She doesn't carry anything but a little knife."

"A knife? You didn't mention any knife when I said we should talk to her."

"I kind of forgot. They all do it. Cindy's family."

I glanced sideways at her. "You know what really happened to her brother, don't you?"

Her chin jerked in my direction. "What do you mean?"

"Cindy said she'd tell the police it was you who did it."

"She's crazy. You don't do what she wants, she beats the hell out of you or does stuff to get even. She hated Robbie, but she thought I should like him." She shuddered. "He smelled."

"You forgot the question." I made my voice calm. "What really happened down there Sunday morning? The truth. Who did you see?"

"Nobody, I told you."

"Was your grandmother down on the dock that day? Just before I got there? Or," I took an unhappy breath, "your dad, maybe? He was here in town."

For a second she just sat there, not moving, and then she said in a small voice, "You *know* what happened. Robbie did it to himself."

"Maybe." I turned down our street "What are you going to do about Cindy?"

"Nothing. She hates the police; she won't tell them anything."

"Was that her car, the green Ford?"

"Yeah, why?"

"Because Chaz was driving it on the bridge." I slowed down. "Listen, this business about the journal is apparently tied to the video project I've been working on and Robbie is . . ."

"You listen! You think you know so much."

Her sulky voice shot up about fifteen decibels. "Fuck Robbie and all the rest of them. You think my dad likes you? Well just forget it. He says all that stuff to everybody, but he won't get married. Not even to the rich one he lives with. She just thinks he will."

"I don't know what you're talking about."

"I saw you! Sitting in the dark the other night."

I pulled the car to a stop in front of the house. "He dropped me off at the house, so?"

"Oh, sure. It doesn't take that long to drop anybody off. And now you think you know all about him, but you don't. And you think I'm just saying it because I'm jealous or something." She opened the door and jumped out of the car. "He thinks so too! Fuck him too!" The car door banged shut and she ran up the sidewalk.

I was too tired to put the BMW away. I left it on the street and limped up the sidewalk, trying not to put too much weight on my foot and ankle. Jerricha had managed to spoil a very warm memory, the memory of Tom Roddler murmuring, "Don't count me out."

I had nearly reached the back door when I heard a familiar sound. Somebody was bouncing a ball in Alec's basketball court. I hesitated, then limped across the street, down the driveway and through the gate in his wood fence.

There was barely enough glow from the streetlight to see him, standing ten feet back from the basket—shorts and no shirt—swooshing the ball through the net over and over, moving just enough to retrieve it when it bounced back his way. As I watched, he sunk it three more times.

"It's almost midnight," I said to the back of his head.

"Yeah." He bounced the ball and prepared to shoot again.

"Are you home now?"

"I guess. Wanna play some one-on-one?"

"No." I turned and pushed open the gate. "I usually need a little more light on my game."

"Yeah?" He glanced over his shoulder at me. "You didn't seem to need much a couple nights ago."

182 False Impression

I shook my head. "What is this preoccupation everybody has with my social life? You waiting up 'til I got home?"

"Nope, just sitting up on the patio, doing some thinking. Roddler's got a reputation for being slick." He threw the ball up at the basket and watched it slide through. "And using people. He used to live around here. Before he traded up to Palm Beach."

I took a steadying breath. "Thank you for your concern. Nothing better than unsolicited advice. Especially from someone who's foolproof in relationships himself."

"Hey, I made a mistake."

"More than one."

He bounced the ball a couple of times. "So what happens now?"

"You'd have to be clearer than that."

He stopped bouncing and stared at the fence. "I screwed up."

I nodded. "You see a pattern there?"

"Nope, I think I finally got it this time." He paused and shook his head. "You think, *The sex is so good—so much better than anything else—it must be the right thing.* So you hang in . . ."

"Stop." I raised a palm. "My self-concept is practically nil at the moment. If you keep it up I'll have to step in front of a bus."

"I didn't mean that. I'm trying to tell you I just finally got it. The rest is never going to be good, no matter how hard you work at it. That's what I mean."

I took in a tired breath. "Look, I make an effort not to get burned on the same stove twice, but you keep a two-handed grip on the burner. That's not a winning combination."

"Hey, everything's a trade off. You make mistakes." His voice was suddenly angry. "I'm not some sixty-year-old guy who can go for weeks at a time without it."

"Neither is he."

I didn't know whether it was true or not, but it gave me great satisfaction to say it.

Chapter 27

I was tired, I hurt in too many places, and all I wanted was ten hours of uninterrupted sleep. Instead I got Bear, wearing a towel and a pair of flip-flops, waiting for me at the mezzanine door.

"Be ready at seven tomorrow morning," he ordered. "I'm going to show you how it happened."

My eyes strayed to the bottom of the towel. "How what happened?"

"I figured out who killed Robbie Garcia."

"Oh." I groaned. "Not tomorrow, maybe Monday."

"Nope, Sunday. Just like when you found him."

"Give me a rain check, okay?"

"You gotta be there. You found him." Bear waved a hand impatiently. "You put me on the right track, talking to people

183

who knew him: teachers, other kids."

That was just to get you out of the third-floor bathroom, I thought with regret.

"I found out a lot of things at the high school, including the kid's nickname. Elmer Fudd."

A yawn hit me mid-frown. "Elmer Fudd?"

"Remember Bugs Bunny? Elmer Fudd said wabbit instead of rabbit and wady instead of lady—and so did Robbie Garcia. His speech therapist said it was an emotionally based problem and he'd probably never get over it. Anyway," he said as the towel slipped slightly, "the point is, you have to go, to run through the whole thing."

I could see he was going to stand there until he got what he wanted. I yawned again and played my ace. "Okay, if Jerricha goes, count me in."

"No problem, she's cool."

"She is not. She won't even discuss it."

"Hey, when I told her it had nothing to do with her family . . ."

"But it does. You said she saw somebody she knew."

"That was before I figured it out." He turned and started up the stairs. "Seven. Don't forget."

At 7:25 the next morning, after way less sleep than I need to survive, Bear and I stood together at the top of the Riverwalk steps.

"I'll show you exactly how somebody knifed the kid and then disappeared right in front of you," he said with authority.

My kindest thought was that he was full of shit and theater. Mostly shit. It was hard to believe that only a week had passed since I stumbled over Robbie Garcia. It was just as muggy, just as still and just as hot; the heat index was already ninety-five. Nita had refused to join us, and Kenji and Jesse were nowhere in sight. I had allowed myself to be coaxed out of bed on a Sunday morning, without benefit of coffee, for a Bear Ego Production, and I was not happy.

Jerricha was at the picnic bench up in the park in the same white shirt she had worn last Sunday, and I had already done my famous walk to the top of the Riverwalk steps and stared at the Trimaran. The only difference between today's charade and the real thing was the absence of heat haze. The sun was flashing blinding, gold rays out of a slightly orange horizon and the whole lost-in-the-fog feeling of the week before was gone.

Bear punched me on the shoulder. "Okay, Keegan, down the steps."

I took in a deep, hot breath, ignored a man and his dog, both of whom stared hard at me, and descended. Four steps down, I hesitated in the spot where I had noticed Jerricha sitting over in the park then turned my head and hurried on down to the band platform. I walked to the edge of the bandstand, sat down and stared at the river.

After a few minutes, Bear called, "Okay, next move," and I got up, plodded down the Riverwalk and hung a reluctant right onto the pier. I knew my steps slowed, but I couldn't help it. Sweat rolled down my neck and pooled in my bra.

"Okay!" Bear shouted from up in the park. "That exactly the way you did it?"

I nodded yes, and he yelled, "Come back!"

"But . . .?" I pointed a questioning finger at the end of the pier.

"No! Come back!"

When I got there, Bear was pacing the Riverwalk, and Jerricha sat dangling her legs off the seawall next to him.

She'd left the white shirt hanging off one corner of the picnic table, and that was a serious error. The top she wore under it was so tiny it barely covered her nipples. She grinned as I sat down beside her. Apparently, she wasn't mad at me anymore.

"Do you get it?" Bear was excited. "You never looked to your left. You went down the steps and never looked left at all until you turned to walk to the pier."

I yawned to show him how exciting that was. "So?"

"Jerricha never looked left either. She read the paper until you came, and then she watched you. For nearly three minutes neither one of you looked toward the pier."

I eyed him. "That's not long enough for somebody to run down it to the boat dock, stab somebody and run back. Especially if he's trying to be quiet."

"No," he agreed, "but it's long enough for a guy out there in waders—who's already stabbed somebody—to walk through shallow water and disappear in the heat haze farther down."

"You're talking about the fisherman, Louie Janclowski," I said slowly. "Why would he do that? He didn't even know Robbie Garcia."

"Yeah, he did. I told you he had a daughter who got mixed up with drugs," Bear flashed a look at Jerricha. "She died from an overdose five years ago this month, and Janclowski swore he'd get even with whoever gave her the stuff. They quoted him in the newspaper." He paused. "I looked in the yearbooks when I was at the high school. His daughter and Robbie Garcia are two pictures apart, and the kid was a known dealer even then."

"But Louie's the one who called the police."

"So? He wouldn't be the first guy to try and take the heat off himself. The police never found a weapon, and Janclowski carried a fish bucket out to the end of the pier when he went to look at the body. If he tossed a knife, one of those fold-up jobs, under the mackerel in his bucket, you'd never see it. Hell, he could've tossed a few cookies in there too, if he wanted. The smell of fish covers anything else. I bet the cops never checked the bucket."

"Robbie didn't have a fold-up," Jerricha remarked idly. "He had a great-big knife."

Bear glanced at her. "Whatever."

I was surprised how much I didn't like it. "What happened to your theory about the guy who lived on the Trimaran? The one who killed Robbie and swam to shore?"

"Turns out it was Robbie living on the Tri. I found his wallet the second time I went down there. Look, I've got one more thing to show you. One more way it might have happened." He raised a hand, waved, and a disembodied head rose slowly up over the end of the pier."

An icy chill shot across my sweaty back, then melted away when I saw the head was attached to a live body: Kenji's. As we watched, he reached down, picked up a bicycle and set it up on the pier. Then he jumped on and peddled rapidly toward us. When he got to the Riverwalk proper he leaped off, ran the bike up the sidewalk to City Hall and disappeared.

"See?" Bear was jubilant. "Thirty-five seconds, and you didn't hear the rubber tires on the planks at all. The sidewalk splits at City Hall; half of it curves around to the top of the park and the other half goes to the parking lot. Forty-five seconds, max, and you're completely out of here."

I narrowed my eyes at him. "And ten seconds later you're up in the park asking Louie and me what happened?"

"Right."

"Chaz was riding a bike. Oh, I get it—Chaz!" Jerricha's eyes lit up. "But I didn't see a bike down there."

"Of course not." Bear's voice was smug. "He laid the bike in the rowboat; he could have stacked three bikes in it, and you wouldn't have seen them from where you were sitting."

"But you'd see something," I protested. "A flash off metal. Something."

"No sun that morning, remember?" Bear said. "All he needed was for nobody to look his way for forty-five seconds."

I could see Jerricha liked the Chaz solution. So did I, but I still held a grudge about the bridge.

Jerricha appeared to be thinking deeply. "Well, that would explain a lot of things . . ."

"Like?"

She sat up straight, straining the tiny top further still. "I didn't want to tell, but I guess I better. See, Robbie called Cindy that morning—in the night, really. He said he took the journal out of her closet and he wouldn't give it back unless she brought him the batch of cookies that she and Chaz were going to sell."

"For crying out loud!" Bear snapped at her. "Why didn't you tell anybody? What were you thinking?"

Jerricha flinched at his tone and deflated a little.

I took a breath and altered the words massed on my tongue to something less punitive. "Why didn't you say anything, Jerricha?"

Her voice was almost a whisper. "I was scared. Cindy gets so crazy, and I didn't want her beating me up. She likes hitting people."

"How do you know Robbie called her?" I asked.

"I listened in." She looked embarrassed. "I just wanted the book back. Everybody knew Cindy had it; she bragged how much it was worth. Robbie said for her to walk down the pier at the Riverwalk and he'd trade her even up. He said not to tell Chaz or it was no deal. Cindy said she'd think about it, and he said think hard or he'd give it to the old lady and Cindy wouldn't have a house any more. She got really nuts and slammed down the phone. I jumped back in bed and pretended to be asleep, and she came in and told *me* to do the trade. She and Chaz were gonna follow and see where Robbie went and take back the cookies. She said Robbie was too stupid to do it right."

"So you came down here?" Bear still sounded aggravated.

"Yeah, and I thought they were right behind me."

"What do you mean *thought*? Did they follow you or not?"

"Well, they were supposed to give me a head start. I got a coffee on the way and a newspaper out of, um, somebody's front yard so I wouldn't look weird while I waited, you know, sitting here by myself. But they didn't come, so after a while I walked down the street to look for them, and when I got back to the table . . ."

"The cookies were gone." Bear's face was smug.

She goggled at him, and he grinned and said, "Because while you were gone, old Chaz took them, rode his bike down the pier, fought with Robbie and stabbed him. He grabbed the diary, but the cookies went every which way in the fight. And then you . . ."

"I didn't know what to do, so I sat at the picnic table and waited," she glanced at me, "and then you came."

Bear nodded. "And Chaz panicked when he saw Keegan. He didn't care if Jerricha saw him, but an outsider was trouble. When Keegan sat down and stared at the river, he grabbed his bike and got the hell out."

Jerricha was blinking at us, tears in her eyes. "I know I shoulda said something, but they—they tore up my room at Cindy's. And broke into Jesse's porch! I kept telling myself I didn't know anything about it, and after a while I kind of forgot I did."

I frowned at her. "But if Chaz took the diary from Robbie, how'd you end up with it?"

She drew in a breath and let it slowly out. "He dropped it

when he gave me the pills and told me to shut up. I picked it up. He didn't even know he lost it."

"But you didn't have it in the park—or at the police station."

"No, I went in Spike O's and asked the guy behind the counter to keep it for me. In case Chaz came back."

"Pretty smart."

"He kept something else for me once. After I talked to the police, I went back and got it."

"I didn't see it at Spike O's later on," I said, thinking back.

"I stuck it in the back of my shorts. I kept my shirt on so it didn't show."

"And then I walked you back to Cindy's house . . ."

"And I put it in my back pack when you weren't looking."

I stared at her, thinking that her father had probably been right. Whatever trouble she'd had with academics in school, she was no dummy.

"Well, it wasn't hers," Jerricha protested. "I did the right thing."

Bear was still figuring out the angles. "Was there blood on Chaz when he dropped the diary? Any marks or scratches?"

Jerricha shook her head. "I don't think so."

"Now what?" I said to Bear. "What do we—you—do?"

"Go talk to your tame detective, I guess." He had a surprised look on his face, as if he wasn't sure what to do about being right.

I turned back to Jerricha. "What are you going to do now?"

"I don't know." She looked miserable. "I don't want to make trouble for my dad. I hate it when people get mad at me."

She started crying, big, soundless tears that fell out of her eyes onto her bare neck, and right on cue Jesse appeared beside her. He didn't seem to care whether she made any sense or not, and after Jerricha fell off the wall into his arms, he called her something that might have been *baby* and said he was taking her home.

I hadn't seen him that enthused about anything since the day he barbecued six white eggplants for dinner.

Chapter 28

From the journal, March 8, 1943

The sand beneath her feet changed from dry and powdery to damp and firm. Moon streaked the black river with silvery ripples, and the breeze was almost cold on her face.

She wanted to walk there forever, just feeling. That's all there really was. Nothing else mattered. Not your family or the things they taught you, not good or bad or rules or common sense or thinking about a future you didn't have. It was all about, and only about, feeling. Without reaching out, she knew just how close his arm was to hers. The electric thing between them, that sensed connection, was as substantial as the palm fronds stirring in the breeze or the mangroves rooted into the river's edge.

She turned to look at him just as he said, "What are you holding in your hand?"

"Something I found at the beach." She held up the white spiral shell. "I'm going to make a necklace out of it."

"With the beautiful little creature still inside?"

"No, I pried it out. Somebody said they have very low IQs. He never even knew it."

"He doesn't know what hit him, and Florence has the beautiful shell?"

"Exactly." She looked out across the river. "You're going tonight, aren't you?"

He shifted his feet in the sand, prepared for the inevitable, but she surprised him. No tears, no arguments, no "You said" or "You promised," even though he *had* said and *had* promised.

"They think I'm a fool," she said in an indifferent voice. "Lena and Clyde both, just entertainment until you can get out of here. Somebody you'll forget as soon as you're home with your wife and children."

He started to speak, but she went on.

"They're wrong. I knew the minute you walked in the kitchen that night. I'll give you one more chance. One more chance to go away. Somewhere safe where they'll never look until this whole war thing is over."

She could hear the smile in his voice. "Even the world at war is just an inconvenience for beautiful Florence."

"That's right, it isn't even real. It's something stupid selfish men do to everybody else. So you have to learn to be selfish for yourself." She drew in a breath. "You shouldn't go now anyway. You should wait; your friend's in no shape to travel."

"He was free for thirty-seven hours before you and Rennie picked him up. He must be out of Florida before they increase shore patrols and call in the FBI."

"But you don't have to go with him."

"Others would be hurt . . ."

"They wouldn't know. They'd think something happened to you, that you couldn't come back."

"I would know."

"And you'd spend a lifetime being miserable? For other people? Only your body would go back, you know. The rest of you would always be with me. Would that make them happy?"

"I don't know. One must do—"

"You sound like a propaganda movie."

He was quiet for a while, then, "Did I tell you about Sundays? Before the war? They were sacred always, for art, music, climbing mountains, dreams. From now on Sundays will be for you. When I do those things, I will think only of you."

Her breath came in sharply, but she managed a smile.

"Well, then," she took a step and dropped to the sand, pressing her face into his leg. "If that's it, don't waste any more time talking."

A great wave of warmth and gratitude swept through him. "Beautiful Florence. Let's go find a warm place to lie down."

"Rennie's gone in the car. Nobody will come out here."

"Better—safer—inside."

"You're right. Besides, there's a bottle of Rennie's special champagne chilling on the bar."

He wrapped both arms around her. "Only a little. My head will need to be clear tonight."

"Just one then. Just one to us."

Over an hour later Rennie returned home in the Packard. As he drove up the driveway, a 1928 Model A shot out of the open garage door and headed straight for him. A few feet before impact, both cars managed to stop in time, and he could see Florence behind the wheel of the Ford. He got out and went to speak to her.

She was wearing another of the new dresses, and her make-up was faultless. Her eyes glittered in the light of the headlights.

"Where are you going all dressed up?"

"To the USO to dance. Why not?"

His eyes flickered to the house and then back to her. "Is . . . ?"

"He's asleep." Her chin jutted out mutinously. "He says he needs his rest."

"Does he know you're going out?"

"No," she laughed, "and he wouldn't care. More important things on his mind. I'll be back before midnight. Before you go."

"But—"

He broke off as she down-shifted and shot past him. When he got back in the Packard, Clyde spoke from the back seat. "I thought the Ford was out of juice?"

"It nearly is." Lena was sitting next to Rennie, and she turned with a wry smile. "That's what she gets for borrowing my car without asking. I've pushed that junker father than I ever drove it. She'll be calling for somebody to come and get her pretty quick."

Clyde shook his head. "Florence really picks her nights, doesn't she?"

"I started to tell her we'd put the time forward," Rennie muttered, as he drove into the garage. "That plans had changed and we'd have to leave earlier."

Lena pressed her lips together. "Better for him," she said finally. "But there'll be hell to pay when she gets back and finds out."

Chapter 29

After Jesse took Jerricha home from the Riverwalk, everyone scattered: Bear went to the police station, Kenji took off on his bike, and I walked back to the house, got my car and drove over to see Louie Janclowski.

I wasn't sure why I was going, exactly. Bear had settled on Chaz as the guy who stabbed Robbie, and I hoped he was right, but there was something about his other theory, the one about Louie getting even with whoever gave his daughter drugs. That bothered me. I liked Louie; I wanted to hear him say out loud that he hadn't done it. Of course, that was tricky since he didn't know he'd been accused in the first place.

I forgot it was Sunday morning, but Louie wasn't at church, he was out back, at his workshop, sitting in a lawn chair drinking beer.

"Want one?" He said when he saw me come around the side of the house.

"No, thanks. I—no. No, thanks." I moved into his patch of shade and stood, trying to think of a tactful approach; instead, I blurted it out. "I wanted to ask you about Robbie Garcia."

"What about him?" He rested the can on one knee.

"You didn't say you recognized him when you saw his body."

"'cause I didn't."

"But you must have. This is a small town, and he was in the same school class as your daughter."

He didn't change expression. "Lot of people I didn't know then. More now."

"But you knew he was a drug dealer."

He fiddled with the beer can. "Knew what I heard on the news. Small time. What's any of that got to do with your video?"

"Nothing. But they haven't found out what happened to him yet and, well, you and I were down there when it happened. The police are going to be suspicious of anybody who knew him. They might start wondering why you were on the Riverwalk the morning somebody killed him."

A smile quirked the corners of his mouth. "You come to warn me? That it?"

"Not exactly. I don't know." I looked him in the eye. "What was in the bucket you were carrying that morning? Besides fish?"

For a moment he didn't respond, then his mouth split in a less-than-amused grin.

"River water."

"Nothing else? No fish knife?"

He shook his head and grinned some more.

"You know Eileen Coates died?"

"Yeah." He tossed the empty can into a cardboard box,

opened a cooler and pulled out another beer. "I heard about that."

"Seems kind of funny she'd go right now, just when I was talking to her about the old days."

The pop top made a fizzing sound as he flipped it. "She was ninety or better. Not so funny."

"She told me you were smuggling when you were eleven years old," I said cautiously.

"Ten. I was ten when we first went out to get stuff off those torpedoed freighters. It was all going to the bottom anyway. We salvaged it."

"Your parents let you do that?"

"Didn't know about it. Never asked." Another smile. "I used to hold the machine gun and watch for U-boats while they were throwing the stuff down. Fired it once."

"At ten?"

He shrugged. "Different life then."

"But the one Eileen Coates remembered best."

"Maybe." He sipped some beer and stared at my right foot. "I hadn't seen Robbie Garcia, not to know him, since he was a kid." He blinked his eyes, and his mouth bulged as if words were trying to push out. "We—I was older when I got married, and my daughter—we wanted her to be self sufficient, make her own decisions. We turned out okay, all of us kids did. Seemed like she would too. But we musta got it wrong."

"You didn't do anything to him, to Robbie? Did you?"

He cleared his throat. "Nope. Sure you don't want a beer?"

I wanted to believe Louie Janclowski, but the feeling he was hiding something stayed with me all the way home.

Our back door was standing open, and Jesse was in the kitchen helping Jerricha make bread crumbs. She was strutting around in four-inch platforms and a minuscule top, ripping up bread and looking blissfully happy.

"Bear still at the police station?" I said as I got a Diet Coke out of the fridge.

"I guess so." She beamed at me. "Jesse's going to teach me how to make pots on his wheel."

"Throw pots," Jesse corrected. He looked happy too.

"He says I've got in—innate talent."

I'll bet he does, I thought, though I wasn't sure what wiggling your ass had to do with throwing pots. "Let me know when Bear gets back, okay?"

"Sure." She followed me out to the hall. "I'm sorry, all that stuff I said, about my dad, I mean. I was just upset. He's kind of a chick magnet, you know? And sometimes I'm just like—well anyway, I didn't mean it." Her smile made her look like a totally different girl. Maybe spilling your guts was as good for the soul as Catholics said it was.

A dizzying thought hit me as I climbed the stairs: Jesse was pretty out there, but his work was good. What if he taught Jerricha to sculpt and throw pots and she turned out to be good too? She already had the funky artist look. Better yet, what if they got married, she settled down, became famous and made Florence DeLong eat every ugly word she'd ever said about her granddaughter?

I smiled to myself, stretched out on the bed and looked through my photocopies on World War II. While I was waiting for Bear to report in, I'd better figure a way to finish Ken's project without Louie Janclowski. After all, when you've accused somebody of murder, however gently, they probably aren't inclined to do you favors.

I flipped through the magazine articles from the *Sunshine Quarterly* looking for ideas. Maybe the spy station at

Jupiter—the one they called Station J. That was another more-or-less open secret during the war, one where something exciting should have happened but somehow never did. I stopped reading and raised my head to listen. Somewhere in the house I could hear a high wailing sound.

As I rolled off the bed, somebody jerked open my downstairs door and clattered frantically up the back stairs. It was Jerricha; I could tell from the dramatic, sobbing breaths. Jesse was right behind her, and they erupted onto the landing shouting at each other. Well, Jerricha was shouting, Jesse was simply making extra-loud calming noises.

My "Stop it! What's wrong?" got drowned out by shrieks. of "They'll kill her! I know they will! It's my fault and they'll kill her!"

I pushed her into one of my two chairs. "Stop it. Tell me what's wrong."

"Omigod, my dad'll kill me . . ."

Jesse knelt on the floor beside the chair and grabbed both of her hands.

"Who was it? What did they say?" He darted an anxious glance at me. "Somebody called on her cell phone."

I put a hand on top of Jerricha's head, like you would a dog, and for some reason that helped. It reduced some of the crying and she quit sucking in gargly breaths.

"Who called? Was it Cindy again?"

Her eyes were huge. "She said—" she made a gagging noise, and I increased the pressure on her head. "Stop it! Cindy's nuts. What did she say?"

"That her bones were old and she'd stomp them and they'd snap like, like—" she started to gag again. "It'll be my fault—again. I got to go. I got to get to Grandmother's house"

For a second, the thought of Little Red Riding Hood

overwhelmed me. I blinked twice and choked back a laugh.

"Cindy threatened your grandmother. Is that it?"

"She said I didn't give the book back, so they were going to her condo. Her and some guy." She shuddered all over and the wailing sound started up again in her throat.

"Stop it. Calm down," I patted her shoulder. "You don't even like your grandmother."

Jesse gave me an disconcerted look, but Jerricha stopped making noises and stared at me through her tears. "What can we do?"

"Call the police."

"No! My dad . . ."

"Then call your dad."

"I—I'm afraid." She struggled up in the chair. "If it gets in the paper . . ."

"Then I'll call him." I ducked into the bedroom for my purse and keys. "And we'll run out to Little Clam Bay to make sure Cindy's not there. If she is, no big deal. You can just give her your famous soccer kick, and she'll collapse in defeat."

Jerricha gave me a wide-eyed, sick look, and I sighed. So much for lightening the moment.

There was no green Ford parked in any of the spaces next to Florence DeLong's condo, but that didn't mean anything. Cindy could have driven a different car or hitched a ride or flown in on her broom, for all we knew.

I parked in an empty space and turned to Jerricha. "Okay, your dad's still not answering his cell phone, and your grandmother didn't believe you . . ."

"She said she'd 'let anyone into her home she pleased,' " Jerricha mimicked, "and to stop being stupid. Then she hung up on me."

False Impression

"Okay," I took another look around the parking lot, "then I guess we knock on her door and see if she's all right."

Jesse rubbed a knuckle against his mustache. "Why don't you two go? I'll wait out front and watch out for Cindy."

"She's gonna be really mad," Jerricha muttered at me, "for showing up. And bringing you."

Well, of course she was. That's why Jesse wasn't volunteering to go in the first wave.

I walked up the sidewalk to Mrs. DeLong's door with Jerricha lagging farther and farther behind.

"Hurry up." I punched the doorbell several times, but nothing happened. I counted ten, punched it again, and Tom Roddler swung the door open. He looked as surprised as I did, but the surprise quickly became a frown.

"What's the problem?" He stepped outside and pulled the door almost shut behind him. "Everything all right?"

"No, it's not," Jerricha blurted. "Cindy called—you know, the girl that used to work for grandmother—and I'm like . . well, she said—she said . . ."

When he didn't stop frowning, her voice faded and her eyes dropped to her shoes.

I was suddenly tired of the two of them and spoke up. "Cindy threatened to stomp your mother's 'frail bones,'" I told him, "among other things. Mrs. DeLong wouldn't listen, and Jerricha knew you wouldn't want the police. We came to make sure she was all right."

Tom Roddler's lips compressed until they almost weren't there. "I don't think there's any reason to worry."

Jerricha pulled at my shoulder bag. "Where is it? I want to give . . ."

"Here." I took out the red diary, now wrapped in a plastic bag, and handed it over. She whirled around, pushed past her father and disappeared through the door. He frowned at me, hesitated, and then followed her, and after a second I went too. Mostly to make sure Grandma actually got the book.

Mrs. DeLong was in the room where she'd served me tea, and I stepped through the doorway into a very weird tableau. Tom Roddler had paused just in front of me, Jerricha stood in the middle of the room, diary in one hand, plastic bag in the other, and her grandmother sat in a chair near the window. All three were staring at the person sitting across from Mrs. De-Long: good old Cindy Meir.

Cindy was gripping a pale-blue, rhinestone-studded purse like she wanted to strangle it, and her eyes were fastened on the red journal.

I grinned at the frustrated look on her face and broke the silence. "Busted, Cindy."

Her eyes shifted to me and then to Mrs. DeLong. "Doesn't matter. I have copies."

Florence DeLong rose and took the book out of Jerricha's hand. "You had it all the time."

"No, she didn't." I said. "Tell her how you ended up with it, Jerricha."

Jerricha tried, but she made a mess of it, slaughtering helpless pronouns and other parts of speech indiscriminately. Eventually she got to Robbie Garcia and the swapped cookies and Chaz dropping the book on the street.

"You liar." Cindy was so furious she glowed. "I never told you to go down there. You swiped it out of my closet." She stopped and shifted her focus to Florence DeLong. "Anyway, I need some money. Your choice."

Mrs. DeLong paid no attention. She paged through the red book, holding it as carefully as if it were the Holy Grail.

Tom Roddler glanced uneasily at his mother, then at

Cindy. "I don't have much cash on me."

"Whatever. I'll take a check."

"If you don't mind," he interrupted, his eyes shifting to me, "I'm afraid this is a family matter."

"No!" Jerricha's voice came from behind me. "I want her to stay. I want somebody here who likes me."

"Don't be ridiculous—" her father began.

There was an odd noise and a cry of protest, but this time it wasn't Jerricha doing the drama-queen stuff, it was her grandmother.

Cindy Meir, chunky or not, was not slow. She snatched the diary out of Florence DeLong's hands, smacked Tom Roddler with her pale blue bag and rushed past me out of the room.

Chapter 30

Florence DeLong slumped in her chair, stunned. The rest of us, after a mega-second of silence, converged on the front door of the condo, trying not to knock each other over.

Outside, Jesse was prying himself out of an ixora hedge, and Cindy was halfway across the parking lot, legs flying, headed in the direction of the condo's marina. Tom Roddler started to run after her, then halted, muttering, "I can't be . . ."

Whatever it was he couldn't be remained unvoiced. Jesse began picking orange flower clusters off his clothes—no help there—and Jerricha was as motionless as a rabbit caught in somebody's kitchen garden.

If I'd stopped to think, even for a second, I'd have let Cindy go, but I was disgusted. Not just at the ballsy way she pushed everybody around but at the way they allowed it. I hot-footed it across the lawn after her, but she was a lot faster than she looked, and my foot and ankle were killing me. By the time I rounded the corner to the backyard, she had reached the docks and was waving frantically at a motorboat a few hundred yards out. No wonder we hadn't spotted her car in the parking lot; Cindy had arrived by water.

She ran the length of the dock, stopped and turned as she heard my feet pounding the planks behind her. The look of incredulousness on her face was almost funny. She jerked around to check the boat's progress, then hustled back to meet me.

"What the fuck're you gonna do?" She almost spit in my face. "Talk me out of it? It's not your book anyway. Crazy old woman, screwed up kid, tight-ass son. World's full of people like that, superior, above-it-all losers, all of them. Not enough guts to get what they want—not enough to even ask for it. Y'all make me sick." She waggled the journal in the air with one hand and slapped me, quick and hard, across the mouth with the other.

I staggered backward, more appalled than anything else. I don't know any women who beat up on people, and I'd never believed Jerricha's stories about Cindy's violence.

I did now. Cindy was like a family cat that runs away, lives in the wild for a couple of years and can't re-adjust to civilization. The only thing that brings them back to humans is regular feedings and not having to fight off rats after dark. I took another involuntary step backward, and she pushed forward into my space and smacked me again.

Fire burned across my stinging face, fueling humiliation, rage and an unholy desire to kill. I balled up both fists, tried not to notice that Cindy outweighed me by sixty pounds, and let my mind go dead cold. She was right about one thing: None of this was any of my business.

"The book isn't mine." My voice sounded thin, so hoarse I hardly recognized it. "But you're not taking it."

Her mouth continued to smile, and her eyes got even nastier. "Sure I am. And I'm going to pull every fucking hair out of your head besides." She tossed the red book down and turned as Sleepy Eyes nudged the motorboat in next to the dock.

He threw a line around one of the pilings. "You need me?" he said to Cindy.

"Nope, be there in a minute" Cindy turned back and came at me, both hands out like claws.

I sucked in a cart load of air, clasped both hands together and swung them straight at her grinning face as hard as I could. The impact sent her stumbling backward and she landed on her ass. I snatched up the book and ran like the devil was after me. At the end of the dock, I turned for a quick look. Cindy was still in a sitting position, and Sleepy Eyes still held on to the piling.

Jerricha, Jesse and Tom Roddler were more or less where I'd left them. Tom was on his cell phone but folded it as I handed him the red journal. His eyes took in my still-burning face. "What . . .?"

"She's gave it back." I snapped, rubbing the back of my aching right hand.

I could hear the sound of a motorboat throttling up nearby, and half a minute later, one went flying down the river toward the inlet. With luck, that was Cindy, minimizing her losses. Smarter than chasing me back to the condo and beating up all five of us.

Tom Roddler shifted his glance to his daughter, then handed her the journal. "Take this to your grandmother." His voice was sharp, but it softened as he turned to me. "I'll be there in a minute. Would you mind going with her?" His blue eyes stayed with me as I thought about it. Was this no longer a family matter, or had rescuing the red book made me an insider? Finally, I shrugged, followed Jerricha inside and watched her put the diary in Mrs. DeLong's lap.

Florence DeLong looked a hundred years old. She stared at my forehead, but her words were for Jerricha, "How much of this have you . . . ?

"She couldn't read it," I interrupted. "Only Cindy, I think."

"And you?"

I looked straight into her cold, faded eyes, started to explain and thought better of it. "I read it all."

Tom Roddler came into the room alone. He darted an uneasy look at his mother, but he seemed to be speaking to the room in general. "If that girl has copies, she can start some ugly, unfounded rumors."

I shook my head. "She was too anxious to get her hands on the original. Without it, she can't prove she didn't write the stuff herself." I gave him a small, tight smile. "Where are your PR people? In fact, where's the entourage you haul around to deal with things like this? Isn't this a Sherry job?"

"She'll be here in a few minutes," he muttered, "but she doesn't handle my personal business. I—the thing is—"

"I've already forgotten what I read, if that's what you mean, but there's another problem: Robbie Garcia. The police are treating his death as suspicious."

"Nothing to do with us. From what Jerricha said, it was some guy with a tattoo."

"It wasn't."

"Bear said so," Jerricha protested. "He told the police it was."

"I know, but Chaz didn't do it." I turned to her father. "When I found Robbie Garcia on the dock he kept saying 'wadduh . . . wadduh,' and I said I'd get him some." I took a breath. "He died before I could do that."

SANDRA J. ROBSON   209

Tom's frown looked like it might become permanent. "What does that have to do with us?"

"He didn't want water; he was trying to tell me who—hurt him." I looked over at Jerricha. "Robbie had a speech problem, right?"

"Yeah, I guess. They always laughed at him. Even Cindy laughed at him."

"Bear told me about it. He couldn't say an r or an l in words. Still, it took quite a while for me to catch on. Robbie Garcia wasn't saying water, he was saying Roddler."

"He was not!" Jerricha flashed a panicky look from me to her father and shouted, "I didn't see anybody I knew down there. Nobody! I already told you!"

I nodded. "I know you didn't. Robbie wasn't talking about your dad; he meant you. I should have realized this morning when I saw your white shirt fluttering off the edge of the picnic table. You weren't in the park when I turned up Sunday morning; it was just your shirt hanging there. I didn't take a good look because I was bummed and avoiding people. I don't know where you were hiding, but you waited until I went down the steps, rushed to the table and put the shirt on to hide the diary you'd just snatched from poor, old, bloody Robbie."

Tom Roddler's face was incredulous, but his mother merely looked resigned. Maybe she was too tired to do any more controlling. Or maybe she just didn't care.

"You lied about the cookies too. You took them while Cindy and Chaz were arguing and went to trade Robbie for the journal yourself. Chaz went after you when they realized what you'd done, but he was too late. And when Bear jumped in with his theory about the bicycle, you agreed in a hurry because it took you off the hook. What did you want with the book, anyway?"

Jerricha's lip shot out. "Cindy got a lot of money because

of that book, and she wasn't even family. If anybody had it, it should have been me. But I didn't lie. Not about seeing Robbie down there, anyway. He was lying flat in that stupid boat. He jumped up and scared me, and I was like—"

"Stop it. Now." Tom Roddler had finally found his voice. "Don't say anything else, Jerricha. We'll discuss this later."

I kept my eyes on his daughter, but my words were for him. "They'll get the autopsy results eventually. If they find traces of her DNA, it'll be more than a discussion."

"They'll know it was me?" Jerricha dropped down on the piano bench and covered her eyes with both hands. "It wasn't my fault. I dropped the box and the cookies went all over and he was swearing at me in this filthy voice. He was so disgusting, I kicked him in the stomach. And then he got mad and flipped open his knife, and I—I kicked him again as hard as I could, and it just went in him. I grabbed the book, and he growled at me and pulled on the knife. When it came out, blood went out all over him. It almost got on me!" She took away her hands and wailed at Mrs. DeLong.

"He fell down, and I knew what you'd say: 'You did it again Jerricha.' So I wrapped the knife in the plastic stuff off the cookies and ran."

Tom Roddler closed his eyes, and I sat down in the nearest chair. Just like that. Not Louie Janclowski wading around in his fishing boots, bitter and vengeful. Not Chaz escaping on the silent rubber wheels of his bicycle. Just Jerricha and her lucky soccer kick.

Bear was going to be more disappointed than surprised.

Jerricha turned her head and blinked at me. "When I saw you, I ducked down by the seawall, and then I went on all fours the back way up the hill. I sat at the table and pretended to read, and I just kept saying over and over that I was really sitting there the whole time and I didn't know anything about it. After a while, it seemed like the truth."

"But—what did you do with the knife?"

"Dropped it in my coffee cup. I took off the wrapping and put it in the garbage can in front of Spike O's later on. "She looked suddenly guilty."I did lie about Robbie's knife. It wasn't great big, it really was a fold-up."

"But you carried that coffee down to the police station," I protested.

She nodded. "It was an extra large, and they asked me if I wanted more, and I poured some of theirs on top of mine so nothing would show. And took a sip every once in a while. They didn't notice."

Chapter 31

From the journal, March 8, 1943

Florence DeLong entered the kitchen at eleven thirty and tossed Lena's car key on the table. "So, everybody ready for the big night?"

Lena gave her a look just short of a smirk. "Back so early? No fun dancing with the lonely noncoms?"

Florence shrugged. "Plenty of hostesses on. I think I'll celebrate with a glass of champagne." She went out into the hallway, and Lena heard the basement door opening. She braced herself and continued chopping onions.

It seemed like a long time before she heard the sound of high heels running down the hall.

"Where are they? Where did they go?" Florence demanded

as she burst into the kitchen.

Lena turned from the sink. "There's nothing you can do about it Florence."

"They're supposed to leave at midnight!" Her eyes were wild and her words came out in little gasps. "Did they all go together? Did you see them?" She grabbed Lena's arm and squeezed hard.

"I only saw Rennie shutting the passageway door." Lena pulled her arm away. "But I heard him yelling to get going. There was some kind of problem, but he said he'd handle it."

"But they all went? All four of them?"

"Of course, Florence. You knew that when you said good-bye and trotted out to play. Don't pretend it's a big surprise." She paused. "Rennie tried to tell you the time had changed, but you were in too big a hurry to listen."

Florence's' eyes were flat and black in the dim light. She spoke as if she couldn't get it straight. "They went out to the island in Ren's boat? They all went in the boat?"

Lena was impatient. "You know they did. That was the plan. First the boat, then hike across the island to the ocean side and wait for the rubber raft."

"How long ago? How long have they been gone?"

"They went about an hour after you borrowed my car—without asking."

"But that's—that's over two hours."

The phone rang, and Lena reached for the receiver. Her hello broke off before it was completely out, and she grew very still as she listened. She hung up, picked the receiver up again and laid it on the table. Her voice was hoarse. "Did you put some gas in my car? Is that how you got home?"

"Yes, one of the boys got me some, but that doesn't matter a damn now. She glanced down at the black Bakelite phone "Who was that?"

Lena's face was stiff. "Clyde. He says leave it off the hook and get out of here. He says the police will be here any minute and we should take the Ford and pick him up downtown in ten minutes. We have to get to Jacksonville. Or as far as the gas coupons will take us. He says don't wait to pack."

Florence stared at her. "Don't pack?"

"The cops are on their way here *now*! Forget your stupid clothes!"

Florence ignored her. "You go. I have to stay here."

"You are a fool, Florence. Do you want to be interrogated by the FBI? That's who's coming. Get your purse. We'll have to siphon extra gas out of the Packard."

"All right." The girl capitulated suddenly. "But I'm driving."

There was a partial moon out as they stowed the gas can in the trunk and rolled down the darkened lane. Florence shifted into second, swung right onto the dirt road without braking and pushed the foot-feed down. Lena breathed a sigh of relief when they finally reached Main Street then gasped as Florence shifted into third and roared straight through and out of town.

"What the hell?" she screeched. "What the hell are you doing now?"

"I'm going to the island. I've got to talk to Rennie."

"They don't let cars on the island. They'll stop you before you even get on the bridge. And even if you make it, there are guard dogs and men patrolling the beach on horseback. They're looking for enemy spies, and you'll get everybody arrested because you're such a—"

"Shut up! Just shut up. I'll go to Jacksonville with you, but first I have to see Ren."

Lena reached a foot over the gearshift and jammed it down in the direction of the brake. The car shook itself to a halt as Florence struggled with the steering wheel. The engine died, and the partially blacked out headlights heightened the darkness along the river.

"We're going back to pick up Clyde right now," Lena said with a hiss. "Forget Rennie; he's been arrested. How do you think they knew to come and search the house? Why do you think we can't drive the Packard?"

Florence stared at the bugs swirling around the dimmed headlights. "They arrested Rennie?"

"I told you."

"You didn't! You only said . . . what about the others?" Her voice trembled. "What happened to them?"

"I don't know. Clyde said they pushed the raft off, so I guess it reached the sub. He and Rennie were hiking back across the island when they got stopped. He managed to get away. Rennie didn't."

"Both men were on the raft? Both made it to the sub?"

"I told you what I know. Get out of the car, Florence, I'm driving. Hurry up."

"No! I've got to get out to the island. I've got to find out what happened."

Florence reached for the ignition key, then slumped over the steering wheel as the size-five heel smashed down on top of her head.

Lena put the shoe back on her foot, got out of the car and ran around to the driver's side. She was tempted to leave the dark-haired girl by the side of the road; instead, she shoved her limp body into the passenger seat and drove back toward town.

Chapter 32

Tom Roddler, his mother, his daughter and I stood together in Florence DeLong's tiny, congested living room, but we were as far apart as any four people could get. Nobody spoke.

I was still struggling with a mental picture of Jerricha sipping coffee strained through a bloody knife while she chatted with Detective DeCicero.

Eventually, Jerricha got tired of the silence. She pushed her hair away from her face, said "I'm going to find Jesse," and went. Nobody told her not to. Her father, his face expressionless, mumbled something about making a call and went into another room. Mrs. DeLong pointed to a chair and said, "I want to talk to you."

I'd seen that one coming. I ignored the directive and moved to the piano bench Jerricha had vacated. "About what?"

She frowned at me. "Steinbeck was a fool."

Steinbeck. This was probably not going to be the talk I'd expected. "I'm sorry, who?"

She waved an impatient hand. "I have not lost my mind. Steinbeck. The author. He said if you wanted to forget a painful event in your life, you had to start at the beginning and remember every single detail over and over, day after day. He said after a while you remembered the facts of the event but not the emotion and the pain surrounding them." She snorted. "He was completely wrong. I remembered Thomas every hour of my life for sixty years, and the pain never dulled at all. Do you understand that?"

"No," I eyed the red book in her lap, "but there's a lot I don't understand. Most people write journals in the first person. Yours reads like a novel that happened to somebody else."

She sat up in her chair and spoke as if she were countering criticism at a symposium.

"That was how I remembered us: the dark-haired girl, the man, the POW, Rennie, Lena, Clyde." She took in a long ragged breath. "The story came out that way, totally unique, sometimes like I wasn't part of it at all. But it helped every time I wrote it down. You didn't go to therapy back then, not unless you wanted to be labeled insane the rest of your life. People went *away* for a rest." Her voice was bitter. "It was never really a secret when you were crazy; somebody always found out."

I looked at the silver hair and wondered if I'd have liked her any better when it was dark and shiny and she was still undamaged. Probably not. I shifted on the bench. "Frank Roddler wasn't Tom's father, right? Two black-haired, brown-eyed people don't make a blue-eyed, blonde child. And I doubt if it was Harold DeLong."

She looked at me incredulously. "Of course not. I never cared for Harold. I only married to give Tom a father."

I shook my head slowly. "I doubt it. I expect you married to get away from the East Coast. The FBI rounded up your buddy Rennie and several of his other friends. You were afraid they'd trace you eventually, so you buried yourself in Oklahoma with a new name and hoped for the best. And then you paid for it."

"It was a terrible time. You couldn't possibly understand. Clyde and Lena hid out in the Carolinas with relatives, and I managed to get space on a train for Providence. I met Harold there; he was being discharged from the navy. I was Jerricha's age, and it was up to me to save my son. Even Oklahoma didn't seem far enough when I heard about Rennie. Something terrible happened to him."

"I know. He died in jail; he committed suicide."

Her head snapped around. "How could you know that?"

"Eileen Coates told me. I just didn't understand her at the time."

"Oh, Lena. Stupid woman. I took care of her for years. Clyde too until he died. They were living back here when I bought the house in the sixties, but they didn't 'put the bite on me' until Clyde had a stroke and she couldn't take care of him."

A bleak smile came and went on her face. "Eileen was very close mouthed when she was young, but when she got old, she blathered on about everything. Most people thought she was crazy, but that boy from the college actually listened to her. He wanted to feature her in his stupid film."

"So you had some friends hang him upside down out the window of his condo?"

"Of course not. He kept calling me up, asking a lot of questions that were none of his business. I merely told Cindy I wanted it stopped, and she took care of it."

"But why? Why bother about a piddling junior-college video? Even if Mrs. Coates told everything she knew, it wouldn't matter. Nobody cares about some sixty-year-old fling—even with a Nazi."

"Thomas wasn't a Nazi!" Her voice was sharp. "And you know nothing about it. Do you know what the French did to their own women back then? The ones they called collaborators? They shaved their heads and stripped them naked and paraded them through the streets." Her voice trembled. "The Forties were not a more innocent time. I did what I did, and I'm not ashamed of it, but my son will not suffer for something he knows nothing about."

"None of that would keep him from being elected state senator. Not today. If anything, the public might think it was romantic."

"The public!' She snorted.

"Are you sure you weren't worried about something else Mrs. Coates might tell? Something with no legal or moral statute of limitations?"

"I suppose you know what you're talking about. I certainly don't."

"Cindy said you rewrote your stories over and over and they ended differently every time."

For a moment her eyes showed confusion. "What does it matter how they ended? The feelings were what counted."

"Yes, but it took me a while to understand. Thomas came ashore here from a U-Boat, and your friend Rennie was hired by the Germans to help him, right?"

Her chin lifted. "Thomas came to rescue two men held prisoner in that awful camp. They were technology experts, captured off a sub, and of course Germany wanted them back. Something about a new airplane design. They weren't Nazis. Rennie wouldn't have helped the Nazis. He hated them."

"And you and Thomas got close, except he insisted on returning to Germany. So you put something in his champagne and went out for the evening and left him in the basement. What did Clyde and Rennie do with the body when they found him?"

A horrified look worked itself across her face. "I would never have hurt him. Never."

I stared into her eyes, trying to see past the lies and self lies, past thousands of handwritten pages about an experience that had lasted only a few weeks.

She glared back. "You don't believe me. Can't you see he's always with me? Now as much as in nineteen forty-three? He never left me, not really."

"Oh, I believe that. He's always been right here. That's why you came back to Florida and bought Rennie's house and stayed in it all these years. And why you repainted the pirate pictures on the wall when they faded. To remember what he looked like."

"I never had a picture of him." Her voice softened. "It was too dangerous."

"And you called the people who bought the house and told them to fill the basement in immediately, right? Or you'd sue them for breach of contract and raise hell in general. You didn't want anybody digging around out there so you hired Chaz and his buddy to guard the place with a shotgun."

"Not me."

"Oh, right, not you. Cindy again. Cindy who'd do anything to protect her free house and lucrative rent."

"It was her duty. She caused the trouble, anyway. Talking to that boy when he came to interview me. Meeting him for a drink and hinting about a scandal. The lowest kind of low class, and too big for her boots besides. I told her to straighten it out or there wouldn't be any more money." She waved an unsteady hand. "But she was stupid. Sent that boyfriend of hers to break into your porch in broad daylight with a house full of people. And then to throw you off the bridge."

"But that wasn't your doing either?"

"Certainly not. I just wanted you to stop asking questions. I am not a young woman. It was all I could do to sell the house for our son. Thomas told me we didn't need it anymore and would soon be together. It wasn't imagination either," she said fiercely. "Every time I wrote in the books I could feel him here, touching me. I've slept with his T-shirt every night since he left me. It was one of Rennie's, but Thomas wore it. It smells just like him." She gave me an almost shy look. "Would you like to see it?"

"No." For a second I felt nauseated. "I don't say you didn't love him, but it wasn't enough to stop you putting something in his drink. And when you got back from the dance and found him gone, you panicked. That's why you kept asking Eileen Coates if they *all* went. You knew he was dead, but he wasn't in the basement. So you had to get to Rennie to find out what he'd done with the body."

"You're a fool too." Florence DeLong laughed out loud, her voice suddenly younger and stronger. "People look their whole lives for that kind of love and don't find it. But I did—in a basement in no-place Florida. I couldn't tell where his body stopped and mine started—and he was going to give that away! I had to do something."

"Like poison him."

"Of course not. Not on purpose. That's why I wanted to talk to you. You read what I wrote. I thought you'd understand. I could never tell anyone, although Lena probably guessed. And I've never been able to write the real end because it always changes. It always turns out some other way."

"I don't . . . what are you saying?"

"It was to make him sleep. Just sleep. I went to the dance because I didn't want to be here when all the yelling started. I knew they'd have to leave him behind. By midnight they wouldn't have been able to wake him up."

"But Rennie moved the time up."

Her voice dropped to a whisper. "They took him along. He couldn't stay awake, and there were patrols everywhere. They dragged him the whole mile across the island to the ocean, but he fell out of the raft on the way out to the sub. They couldn't risk a light and," she sobbed audibly, "they lost him. I didn't know until I came to in the car on the way to Jacksonville and Clyde told me the whole story. He blamed me for all of it. Me!"

She started to get up and then dropped back down again. "You know what all those therapists used to say to me? 'Live in the moment.' Live in the damned moment. Not one of them saw that I was living in the moment my whole god-damned life."

I left Florence DeLong alone with her red book and went out to the car. I had a great desire to go home, stand in the shower and drink straight shots of Tequila. I walked quite a way in the wrong direction before I realized I didn't remember where the car was. Then I turned and stumbled the other direction.

Tom Roddler appeared beside me and took my arm. I let him have it, but it wasn't a comfort.

After a while he said, "So where is he? Under the basement floor? In the river somewhere? Or safely at home in some little town in Germany disliking his grandchildren as much as she dislikes hers?" His voice was bitter.

"How long have you known?"

"I found the diaries under her mattress when I was eleven. I thought . . . I thought all that writing was making her sick. The same stories over and over, changing one word one time, another word the next. Years later I read them again and realized my stepfather wasn't my real dad. I always thought he probably was. We were a lot alike."

"Did he know?"

He nodded. "He read them too."

"But he didn't say anything?"

"Not to me. He was too busy trying to die with dignity."

"How do you know she didn't change the facts around too? While she was finding better words?"

"I don't." He made a noise in his throat. "A few years ago, when I decided to get into politics, I hired somebody to look into it."

"And?"

"The history part's accurate. They kept a lot of secrets in those days, and the government leaned on the newspapers to keep quiet about local spies and the POW camps. Some eighteen-year-old kid and a few other prisoners managed to escape from Camp Blanding a few times, but that was in north Florida. The kid hung himself."

"What about the U-boats off Seminole Beach?"

"Lot of stories. One supposedly surfaced near Jupiter Island, and a German sailor waved a pack of Lucky Strikes. Two locals with the Civil Air Patrol claimed they landed their planes out on the barrier island and heard men calling to each other in German. That kind of thing. There are only two documented cases of Germans making it ashore, and they were caught almost immediately."

"What about her house? Rennie's house?"

"Built by a Chicago banker, sold to a European holding company in nineteen thirty-nine, title transferred to Reinhold Hauser in nineteen forty-one, seized by federal authorities in nineteen forty-three. Resold to a doctor after the war, bought by my mother in nineteen sixty-one."

"And the SS Buccaneer?"

"Nobody knows. Believed to have sailed to Cuba, been refitted, name changed, et cetera"

"So there's no proof of any of it, really. Not with Eileen Coates dead?"

He looked at the ground. "No proof there either. She was diagnosed with dementia years ago."

"Then you weren't really worried about Cindy at all."

"Of course, I was. Am. You never know what the public's going to do." He stopped walking. "Are you going to tell me what happened to my father?"

I stopped too and turned to face him. He was a great looking guy, tanned face, crinkles around his blue eyes, easy smile. If he was anything like his dad, I could almost understand Florence DeLong pulling out all the stops to keep what she was losing. At the moment his eyes were bleak and a little more gray than blue, making no attempt to charm or influence me. He had asked, now he simply waited.

So I told him.

He didn't say thank you or anything else. He took my arm again and led me to my car, which had been in plain sight all the time.

"Can we get together in a couple of days? When I can think?"

"I thought you were living with somebody."

"No. You've been listening to Jerricha, who thinks I can charm the pants off anybody. Look, I'm not the best guy in the world. I've done a lot of things nobody would be proud of and will probably do more. But it's been years since I sat out in front of somebody's house and talked. Never mind two hours' worth. My daughter doesn't know everything."

"About Jerricha . . ." I began.

"That's what I have to think about."

He opened the door and put me in the front seat, leaned down and kissed somewhere between my ear and my neck. As he straightened up, a black Lexus drove up beside us. Sherry reached over to open the passenger door and glared across the leather seat at me. Tom opened his mouth to say something else, changed his mind, and got in the Lexus. Before he even had a chance to buckle up, old Sherry was laying rubber out of the parking lot.

Chapter 33

I garaged the BMW and limped along the sidewalk to our back door. I felt like I'd been beaten with a club and left to die. The back door was locked, but eventually I found the key on my ring and opened it.

"Hey, Keegan!"

I looked up and across the street. Alec was leaning against the decorative railing on his second floor patio, waving an arm at me. "I got martinis. You look like you need one."

"I need a bath," I called back before I thought.

"Okay. Come over afterward. I'll make a new batch."

I wasn't going to, but I nodded to avoid a discussion and went inside.

The kitchen was dark and empty. It was a toss-up whether there'd be any dinner tonight or if Jerricha ever cooked for us again. A toss-up whether she'd get nailed for Robbie's murder. If they could keep her mouth shut, she probably wouldn't.

Even if there were DNA evidence, the right kind of lawyer would play hell with it. He'd claim she simply met or touched Robbie Garcia sometime before he went down on the dock. Unless detectives had searched the garbage can in front of Spike O's the day Robbie died, they'd missed their chance to find any of his blood on anything she'd touched. And he'd pulled the knife out himself. Lucky old Jerricha.

I showered and shampooed my hair and blew it dry and put on clean shorts and a tank top. No bruises or slap marks were showing on my face at the moment, so I skipped make-up. It was only when I caught myself sliding into my sandals that I realized my physical body was actually thinking of crossing the street and drinking Alec's martinis, no matter what my moral, mental and emotional body had in mind.

I went down the steps to the side porch and looked across the street at Alec's house. The patio looked the same: same rusted grillwork, same dying plants, same Alec waiting with martini glass in hand. I was all cleaned up with no place to go, and I did not want to sit alone in the mezzanine thinking over the last few hours.

I opened my upstairs door and stepped out on the landing. The house was quiet except for the *clack-clack* of Bear's old Royal a flight and a half up. In all the fuss, I had forgotten Bear and his trip to the police station. I listened for a few seconds then climbed the stairs to third floor.

Bear's door was open, and he was sitting at a beat-up typing table, no shoes, no shirt, but definitely wearing pants. You never knew for sure.

I leaned against the door jamb. "Still working on your locked-room story?"

He stopped typing. "Yeah, what's up?"

"I came to give you the ending."

"Yeah?" He studied my face, then motioned me to take his chair and went out into the hall. He came back with two open bottles of some dark beer. He handed me one and dropped down on his sleeping bag with the other.

"I got it wrong, huh? It wasn't Chaz."

I took a couple of long, slow swallows of cold beer before I told him. I left out the part about Tom Roddler's real father being a possible Nazi. I didn't want Bear featuring it in one of his books, and anyway, Tom looked a lot like his supposed stepfather. Mrs. DeLong might easily have rewritten that ending too.

"Two perfectly good theories, and both crap," Bear said finally. "And they were both better than the truth. It's too anti-climatic that Jerricha killed Robbie Garcia by accident." He gave me a sharp look. "Or *was* it an accident?"

"Hard to tell, she lies like a rug with fringe. Like her grandma."

"And what about Cindy? She just gets away with it?"

"Probably. She'll say she did what Mrs. DeLong told her: got somebody to steal a nineteen forty-three microfilm and a recorder out of my car, scare trespassers away from a building site, and threaten Joey and me with bodily harm. My word against hers."

"Think she also got her friend Chaz to slip Eileen Coates a few sleeping pills or something just as lethal?"

"Again, hard to prove. Cindy's karma must be a lot better than her brother's. Poor, stupid Robbie Garcia. All he wanted was to trade a book he couldn't read for some cocaine."

Bear grunted and stood up. "Come on, let's go."

"Go where?"

"The beach. No point in finishing the wrong story, and I need a break anyway. You look like you can use one too."

I didn't have anything better to do, so I went downstairs, pulled on a bathing suit under my shorts and top and met him in the garage. When I reached for my car keys, he shook his head. "I'll take Amy's Jeep. Surfboards are already in it."

"I don't surf, never tried it."

"'Bout time then."

We backed out of the garage into the street, and for a couple of seconds, just before Bear shifted into drive, we were looking straight up at Alec. He was still leaning on the patio railing, and our eyes met as he raised one hand in an uncertain wave. I waved back, but by then we were halfway down the street.

The beach was quiet. As we pushed our boards out into waist-deep water, I got a brief lesson on paddling—along with Bear's assurance that effective paddling was too involved for beginners like me anyway. Then we practiced watching for white water and spotting the right wave. When one came our way, Bear yelled "flop face down," and I threw myself lengthwise on my board, hung on and flew straight at the beach, astonished at how easy catching a wave actually was. The next second I went headfirst over the tip of the board as it disappeared from sight. The subsequent surge of white frothy water turned me upside-down, flooding my nose and ears with warm, salty liquid. I came up spluttering and choking and rubbing grit out of my eyes.

"Too far forward," Bear shouted, almost in my ear. "The board went for the bottom. You pearled."

"Pearled, right." I blinked and coughed and he grinned.

"Let's try it again."

I was too short of breath to disagree, but my opinion was, if I couldn't ride the board flat on my belly, there wasn't a prayer I could ride it standing up.

This time I caught the biggest incoming wave, flopped at the right time and flew toward shore with less confidence than the first time. That was good, since I went off the left side almost immediately with roughly the same results as before. When I came gasping up out of the water, a large hand pushed my head back under.

"What the hell . . . ?" I spluttered, fighting my way to the surface.

"Stay under when you pearl," Bear commanded, "otherwise the board'll pop up and crack you in the head."

I lost count of the times I dragged myself out of the surf and trudged back out to try again.

Eventually, Bear told me to stand on the board. "You ought to get up once your first time out. Ever do squat thrusts at the gym?"

"Not lately." I was so exhausted I could barely get the words out.

"As soon as I yell go, flop on the board, get to your knees and just stand up. Doesn't matter how long. Okay?"

When the wave came—a sprawling, great white line that curved higher and higher into a dark blue wall—I did as he said, managed a kind of pathetic pushup, jerked up my legs, bent my knees and . . . I was on my feet. By the time I got that far, the big wave had fizzed to a roller, but for a second and a half I was flying. Until the board came to a halt, and I didn't. I ended up in the shallows again, my bikini bottoms full of wet sand.

Bear hauled me to my feet and dragged me toward shore. "Good. Next time we'll work on your stance."

Stance? What stance? I staggered through the surf and collapsed onto warm, dry sand.

"Not bad at all." Bear dug two beers out of a cooler and twisted off the cap for me. "Here, don't want to dehydrate." He leaned back on his elbows and closed his eyes.

I downed half the beer and lay back, wet hair spread out to

dry. The sun was edging closer to the top of the dune, and the breeze was mild and soothing. Despite the roar of surf, it was very quiet; no inner sarcastic voices telling me how I should or shouldn't have paddled, flopped or even surfed at all at my age. In fact, now that I thought of it, I hadn't heard a single nasty voice since I popped Cindy one on the nose. Should have smacked hell out of somebody years ago.

Bear was apparently reading my mind. "I can't believe you actually bitch-slapped the infamous Cindy. Where'd you learn to do that?"

"Self-defense class. Guy taught us a lot of stuff before they found out and fired him. He was a former Viet Nam vet."

"Oh, the kind that hears voices."

I stiffened, turned my head and stared at him. "You ever hear voices?"

"I got two ex-wives." Bear sounded resigned. "Sometimes I hear whole symphonies. No big deal. It's only if they're so loud they drown out your own that it matters."

"How do you know which one's yours?"

"It's the really quiet one that tells you what you need to do next. And how to handle all the shit that's going to happen when you actually do it."

I thought about it for a minute. "You're probably right. You must be a lot smarter than you look."

"Straight up." Bear finished his beer. "Smart enough to know you owe me."

"For what?"

"For thinking up theories and clearing away all the garbage so you could dope out what really happened to Robbie Garcia."

"You are so arrogant." I shook my head in mock admiration. "What sort of payment do you expect."

He got to his feet, picked up both surfboards and started

toward the parking lot. "You could proof my book when it's done. For free." He flashed a wicked grin over his shoulder. "Unless you have something more . . . interesting in mind."

"Not even a chance," is what I said, but I was smiling as I followed him to the jeep.

Epilogue

Just so you'll know, I finished Ben's project, got the money, paid off my credit card, and the air conditioner is still working.

Finishing the video wasn't nearly as hard as I'd tried to make it. I downloaded material from archive.com, cut some old black-and-white war footage into ordinary scenes of Seminole Beach in the Forties, and filled in the rest with bits of Joey's stuff. Louie Janclowski did four minutes of reminiscing, as if he'd been waiting for the chance his entire life, and I hired somebody who didn't look like Edgar R. Murrow to voice-over Joey's speaking segments and add some new ones. Ben was very pleased when *War in the Tropics* was a mini-hit and the college received the promise of additional grant money.

I told Louie Janclowski about Jerricha, but he didn't seem surprised. After a while he said he knew Robbie Garcia had been staying on the Trimaran because he'd spotted him one day when he was fishing. "I been kind of keeping an eye on him," he admitted. "He had dead coming a long time."

Tom Roddler's campaign for state senator is still in the works, and so far no one has mentioned Jerricha's involvement in Robbie Garcia's death. Tom gets up to Seminole Beach every now and then, and we've managed to spend some time together. When we go out, Sherry doesn't drive us.

Actually, there's been nothing at all in the papers about Robbie's death or Web Boy's accident, and none of us have heard from DeCicero in weeks. Bear, however, has nearly finished his version of the case and handed me several chapters to proof. I guess I'll do it if I can talk him out of his working title: *Bodies in Heat.*

Last week Jerricha ostensibly went to visit out-of-state relatives, but the real word is she's stashed at a rehab center up near Ocala for rich people's kids. The day after she left, Cindy's house burned to the ground.

The fire is under investigation.

Acknowledgments

Thanks:

To John Kennedy, for editorial skills and teaching me to write and think at the same time

To Steve Graff, for information on police procedures.

To Herb Kraft and ChiChi Gonzalez, for their memories of Florida during WWII.

And to my husband, who always offers to help me with the sex scenes.

About the Author

Sandra J. Robson is a speech pathologist and the author of a second Keegan Shaw Mystery, *False as the Day Is Long*, and a self-help book, *Girls' Night Out: Changing Your Life One Week at a Time*. She has lived in London and traveled extensively in the British Isles. She resides on the east coast of Florida with her orthodontist husband.

Visit Sandra's website at SandraRobson.com.

Made in the USA
Middletown, DE
25 May 2016